The Righteous Son

THE LOST DAUGHTERS TRILOGY BOOK THREE

VIOLA TEMPEST

KINGDOM OF PEACE
KINGDOM BAOSHU
HEPI
SHENHUA KINGDOM

ORPHANAGE
JINU KINGDOM
INAJEN ISLAND
N
W E
S

CONTENTS

CHAPTER
ONE

FOR DECADES, THE SEED OF HATRED, OPPRESSION, AND discrimination had been germinating in the soil of Jinu Kingdom. The sorrows and cries for help wafted in the eerie winds, and the kingdom that once flourished with wealth and power was now struggling.

Over the years, the kingdom had lost allies and made enemies because of Qianfan's temper and pessimism. The people of Jinu had migrated to other kingdoms after living in the deteriorating state of their own. The land had gone barren, the soil became unfertile, the water surrounding them had depleted, and with every passing second, the people were losing hope.

The king and queen had turned a blind eye to the deprecating situation of their kingdom. For them, everything seemed normal and perfect... as long as the circumstances did not affect their extravagant lifestyle.

Daiyu, who was once the empathetic soul of the people, was now an overly desirous, self-centered bitch who only cared about herself. And while Qianfan's personality had only gotten more menacing with time, he also managed to become a narcissistic dictator.

The king and queen failed their people, and their feelings for each other had waned, too. The love that Qianfan and Daiyu once had for one another had now turned into pure resentment.

After the birth of their fourth child—a daughter—Qianfan blamed Daiyu for giving him a child that was of no use to him. And the love that Qianfan once had for his third child—his only son—had averted after the first five years.

Daiyu, on the other hand, reprimanded Qianfan for being a monster. He continued to abandon his children, one after another, and forced Daiyu to also turn against them. His actions and words made Daiyu suffer. She blamed him for making her numb, for killing the motherly nature that she once had inside of her. She hated herself for not standing up for her children, for not stopping

Qianfan when she could've, and she couldn't live with the guilt.

She couldn't even find it in herself to love the children she still had with her. How could she stand here and love two of her children when the other two were possibly dead?

Daiyu spent most of her days locked inside her room. Whenever her children crossed her mind, she distracted herself by buying expensive clothes and jewels, spending all her time only on herself. She created a world for herself where she pretended as if her children never existed—that was the only way to keep her mind from bleeding guilt.

At the other end of the castle, Qianfan spent his time away from Daiyu, focusing his own time on whatever numbing drink he could find and building an army of mass destruction. He wanted the other kingdoms to fear him, to see Jinu as the one untouchable kingdom in all of China, and in his mind, he knew that if war were to ever erupt, he'd be ready.

As a couple, Qianfan and Daiyu had failed. They hardly saw each other anymore, and whenever they did, it was *always* an unpleasant encounter.

As parents, they were nothing more than a disappointment.

And as the kingdom's leaders, they had proven to be unsuitable.

Jinhai, the prince of Jinu, was meant to make things right. Qianfan wanted him to be a mirror image of himself. From a very young age, Jinhai was trained to be a fighter—a killer. From fencing to martial arts, he was taught *everything* that was related to violence. For Jinhai, it wasn't that bad; he liked learning new things, and he aced everything that he tried. But when he failed, his father would strike.

Every time Jinhai fell or got injured, he'd cry, and Qianfan *refused* to accept that.

"Boys do not cry," Qianfan would say every time Jinhai shed a tear. "You are weak; you *cannot* be weak."

For the first five years of Jinhai's childhood, he saw the virtuous version of his father—the one who gave him everything and treated him like an actual human being.

But little did he know, happiness never lasted long when it came to Qianfan, lasting only temporarily until he found himself longing for his next fix.

It was Jinhai's sixth birthday when things completely changed. The kingdom was decorated with red dragons and lanterns, as usual—Jinhai's birthdays were always celebrated like festivals. Qianfan distributed gold coins amongst the peasants, and he invited kings and queens from neighboring kingdoms. Daiyu was expecting another child—whom Qianfan expected to be a boy—and the day was meant to bring nothing but peace and joy.

The party began with Jinhai greeting all the kings and their sons. They had dinner together while talking over future plans that all the kings had for their sons and future leaders. But Jinhai never got along with the other princes his age. He found them too shallow and egotistical, and he'd much rather be friends with the children of the townspeople, something that Qianfan always disapproved of as the peasant boys only ever deterred Jinhai from his royal upbringing.

And he was right.

When the party came to an end, Jinhai and the rascals came sprinting down the main hall, where he tripped over the velvet rug and fell. He slammed his head onto the ground, and when he tried to stand up, his vision blurred. All he could make out was the red blood in front of him... *his* red blood. His breathing came to a stop, his lungs seized, and he began to cry.

Daiyu, who was due to give birth in a week, came running to her son's aid. But Qianfan stopped her by grabbing onto her wrist.

"Leave him be. He needs to be strong. Let him deal with this on his own. The maids will help him clean up," he whispered.

"What's wrong with you?!" Daiyu shouted. Everyone in the room shifted their attention toward them.

"Boys are not supposed to cry," Qianfan declared, and the other kings nodded in agreement.

"In dreams of a lion, you have birthed a lamb," one king remarked, and all the guests laughed.

Qianfan hated the insult, but even *he* had to admit —they were right. His weakling of a son had turned Qianfan into a joke. He wanted nothing more than to pretend that Jinhai was never born and start over with a new son, but he couldn't just get rid of him like he had done with Xiuying and Xiaofan. This moron was the future king of Jinu, and someone would definitely notice if he were missing.

"You are a disappointment," Qianfan muttered to his son and walked out, refusing to even look at Jinhai, who was still bleeding on the ground.

The guests soon left, and the evening ended with gossip that was going to entertain their guests for months to come. Qianfan forbade Daiyu to visit Jinhai. She was furious, but her condition didn't exactly allow her to fight against it, so she went to bed with a heavy heart.

Jinhai sat alone in his room that night, surrounded by everything a boy could ever want... except for the support of his parents.

"Where did it all go wrong?" he asked himself as he stared up at the ceiling to admire the wooden carvings. "All my life, I've tried to please my father, and yet, he still hates me. If I'm not supposed to cry whenever I get hurt, what am I supposed to do? Why won't he just tell me what to do?"

The next day, Jinhai woke up with a heavy head. All he wanted was for his mother to be by his side, though she wasn't. He wasn't allowed to leave his room, as per the doctor's order, but he *was* his father's son, after all. He wanted to see his mother, and so he climbed out of bed and marched toward his parents' room. And that was when he started to hear echoes of screams. He slowly moved closer to their room, and the voices became louder—his father was shouting in rage over his mother's wavering voice.

"I cannot tolerate you or your children anymore. You have given me nothing but disappointments!" Qianfan yelled.

"You are acting as if you have compromised your entire life for me. You have done *nothing* for me!" Daiyu yelled back. "You are never happy! You wanted a son so badly that in order to get that, you abandoned *two* of our daughters. Now you have a son, but he's not like how you imagined, so now you're thinking about abandoning him, too! What kind of father are you? Do you even have a heart?"

Daiyu's voice overlapped with the shattering sound of glass. Jinhai flinched. What just happened? His heart started to race, hoping that his mother was okay. He peeked through the door's keyhole and saw pieces of a broken glass vase.

"You will *not* say a word about this," Qianfan ordered. "Next time, I won't miss."

"What else is new?" Daiyu whispered in resentment as she marched toward the door and opened it to find Jinhai standing there. At first, she was startled, and guilt stabbed at her, but the anger and hurt blanketed it.

"What do you want?!" she screamed at him. "You and your siblings have brought nothing but hurt into my life. I wish I'd never given birth to any of you!"

Jinhai's heart sank, heartbroken by his mother's words. She had always been so kind to him, treating him as if he were a porcelain doll. Never in his life had he seen her behave like this, but seeing the anger on her face, he was at a loss for words. He turned around slowly and walked back to his room, where he curled up in bed and wrapped his own arms around himself for comfort.

"How can someone be surrounded by people yet still feel so alone?" he whispered to himself.

Minutes later, his door opened. Jinhai eagerly spun around, hoping to see his mother and run into her welcoming arms. Instead, he found Haitao standing by the door, accompanied by his father, Lixin.

Haitao was one of Jinhai's closest friends. They met two years back in a fencing class and had been inseparable ever since. Haitao lived amongst the peasants inside the kingdom, and his father was nothing more than a mere cobbler. He didn't have any siblings, and his mother had died from an incurable disease several years ago.

They both entered the room, and Haitao joked, "How's your head? Do you still remember me?"

Jinhai laughed and nodded.

"Are you sure you don't have brain damage? Maybe memory loss?" Haitao asked, glancing his friend up and down.

"Yes," Jinhai replied.

"Glad to hear it, my son. Get better soon," Lixin said while patting Jinhai's shoulder. "You are a brave one. You can handle this."

Jinhai smiled and offered Lixin and Haitao a place to sit near his bed.

"Here," Lixin handed Jinhai a covered glass bowl, "I made you your favorite tofu, just how you like it."

"Thank you. It's just what I needed," Jinhai mumbled.

"You don't look so good. Is everything okay?" Lixin asked, his brows furrowed.

"Yes, I'm just lightheaded," Jinhai answered, only revealing half the truth.

"Okay, you should get some rest, then," Lixin suggested.

"No, no, it's fine." Jinhai nearly jumped out of bed with the need to keep them there. "I could use the company."

They all settled in and talked, but after a while, Lixin had to leave for work. Jinhai thanked him again for the tofu, and Lixin left with a bow. Once Jinhai and Haitao were alone, he told his friend everything that had happened. The problems were too big for their tiny minds, and they tried to make sense of the situation, but they failed to do so. All Jinhai knew was that he was hurt because of his parents, and in order to protect himself, he had to stay away from them.

A WEEK HAD GONE BY, AND NO ONE FROM JINHAI'S FAMILY came to see him. But he was fine; he knew how to keep his expectations low so that he wouldn't be disappointed.

Within the week, the news had spread all over the castle that the queen had given birth to a daughter, and the only person who saw this as good news was Jinhai. Daiyu had given the baby girl to a nanny the moment she was born and marked with the stone, and told the nurses that she wanted nothing to do with the child. Under the law, Jinhai was her only child. The child's room was next to Jinhai's, which once belonged to Xiaofan, and her name was Xiaosheng, named by Jinhai himself. After seeing how his mother had abandoned both him and his baby sister, he promised himself that he'd be there for Xiaosheng no matter what.

Jiayi was the name of the nanny who would now look after Xiaosheng. She had been barren her entire life, so when she learned that she'd be taking care of a child—a princess—she was more than thrilled, the best gift that she could ever ask for. She had been married and divorced several times now because of her infertility, but her wish had finally come true.

Jinhai spent his days and nights with his younger sister. He felt protective of her, and he made sure that she was properly looked after and loved. The happiness that Xiaosheng brought into his life made him forget the sorrow that his parents had given him. It made him forget how he had also been injured by them. He looked to Jiayi as his own mother, and he tried his best to forget the evil eyes that he had seen in the queen—the evil eyes of his royal parents whom he would enact revenge upon one day.

THE SEASONS CHANGED, AND THE TREES SAW MANY COLORS, moons, and exquisite sunsets. Fifteen years had passed, yet the memories of his parents still lived inside Jinhai's mind as if they had happened just mere days before. Jinhai was now twenty-one, a tall, broad-shouldered, and handsome-looking man with long black hair, light brown eyes, a heartwarming smile, and a glowing complexion.

Apart from his appearance, his soul was pure. He had grown up to be considerate, empathetic, charitable, and quite the opposite of Qianfan. He had spent years and years gathering the knowledge that would help him make his kingdom a better place. He had not only excelled academically, but had also trained himself in weapons development, mastered martial arts, and often disguised himself as a peasant so he could go into the kingdom and interact with his people to learn more about them.

Over the years, his relationship with his sister had grown strong, and they had become each other's best friend. Xiaosheng was now fifteen, with similar features and complexion as her brother, but much shorter.

Jiayi looked after both of them like they were her own, and they treated her like their mother. They shared their ups and downs with her, and they came to her whenever they failed or succeeded. Daiyu and Qianfan never tried to reach out to them. They would only appear as a family when they were in the public eye. They would laugh and smile in front of the peasants, appearing as a perfect royal family, but behind closed doors, they resented each other.

Haitao and his father, Lixin, had been there for Jinhai during every step of his life. Lixin was like a father to Jinhai. He helped him become a better version of himself, and Jinhai only believed in himself because of the support that Lixin and Jiayi had given him.

Jinhai wasn't the king yet, but he knew that time was near. He was doubtful that his father would give him the crown, but he was certain of one thing—that his people loved him. They saw him strive to improve the kingdom, and when the time comes, they would all stand behind him.

"What took you so long?" Xiaosheng asked as he entered his room after a long day of fishing at the sea.

"Fishing?" Jinhai laughed.

"I was waiting for you. I haven't had dinner yet," Xiaosheng murmured.

"I've told you many times to not wait for me," Jinhai answered in a polite tone as he sat down next to her, and they both started to dig into their plates.

Xiaosheng took a bite before looking up at him. "Got your favorite tofu made."

Jinhai smiled. "Yes, I can see that. Though, the one

that Haitao's father makes just hits different." He chuckled.

Xiaosheng nodded with a slight shrug. "Nothing can beat his."

"So, why the long face? Is everything okay?" Jinhai asked, noticing how Xiaosheng was quieter than usual, and her cheerful smile was missing.

"I don't know. Lately, I've been feeling out of place, useless, like I have no purpose. I keep roaming around the castle like a ghost."

"Well, that's not necessarily a problem. Tell me, Sister, what are your dreams?"

"What do you mean? Are you making fun of me?" Xiaosheng sneered.

"I certainly am not. Everyone has dreams. They are everything a person needs to stay inspired and hopeful. Having a dream makes you want to get up every morning and work for it. It gives your life a purpose. If you have none, you'll feel like you are lost. You'll feel like you're less motivated. A mind that is knitting dreams is less likely to fall to negative thoughts," Jinhai replied earnestly.

"I haven't thought about it that way." Xiaosheng grinned.

"Think about it, then. Find a dream, follow it, and I will be right here to support you every step of the way." Jinhai smiled

"What if I can't do it? I'm not strong like you."

This reminded Jinhai of the time when he felt the same, and Haitao's father made him understand something important. "Xiaosheng, it took me a great deal of time to understand this, and I want you to know that nobody is perfect. Everyone has weaknesses, insecurities, and self-doubts. The best thing you can do is be aware of them. It will help you be less judgmental, more mindful of your actions, and it will help you stay grounded and have self-control. You are saying that you are weak, and that's exactly how you start. You point out your weaknesses, and you work on them, push yourself to overcome them, and become an improved version of yourself. I have weaknesses, too, and sometimes the things that you think are weaknesses turn out to be your biggest strengths."

Xiaosheng smiled. "How do you always have all the answers?"

"It's because of all the experience that I have. I was born six years before you. Have you forgotten that already?" Jinhai quipped.

"Oh, I must've forgotten—the six years when you were just a *child*," Xiaosheng teased.

"Hey, don't underestimate your brother. I had the wisdom of a monk at that age!" Jinhai laughed.

"Maybe," Xiaosheng chuckled, "but I'm going to bed, Sir Wise One."

After Xiaosheng left, Jinhai was left in his room all alone. He felt at peace because he was happy. He could be there for Xiaosheng, and he was relieved that she had a family she could turn to. He was still keeping the promise that he'd made to his younger self.

He woke up early the next morning and began to

prepare for his day. The food drive for the local community was scheduled for this evening. This was something he did every month to connect with the people who needed support, to interact with those who thought the prince was not within reach, and most importantly, he did it for himself. He'd saved all the coins that he'd gotten from his father and the other royal kings when he was born, just for this occasion. He felt like he didn't need or deserve any of it. The kingdom's treasure was more than enough, while the basic needs of the people were hardly being met. It was unfair to them, and if he used the coins for himself, he would never be able to forgive himself.

The door to his room resounded with a knock, and when he didn't reply, it opened. To his surprise, in walked his father, Qianfan.

"My son!" Qianfan exclaimed with excitement.

Jinhai raised his brows at him. "Now you remember you have one? After fifteen years? How about a daughter?"

"Yes, at least I remember, unlike you," Qianfan shot back.

"Why? Are you the only one who's allowed to forget about or abandon people?" Jinhai questioned.

"You are forgetting that you are talking to your father," Qianfan stated flatly, all the pretense of excitement gone.

"A father who forgot that I existed for almost six years of my life," Jinhai corrected. "You cannot choose to become a father whenever it is convenient for you."

"Keep it up, and I promise you will lose the crown that isn't even yours yet," Qianfan warned.

"I'm not worried about that one bit." Jinhai laughed sarcastically as he walked toward the windows to close them.

"The reason why I stopped by was to ask you to *not* do the food drive today," Qianfan confessed, ignoring his son's jab. "It creates chaos and disrupts the roads near the harbor."

"It only becomes chaotic because the people of your kingdom are struggling to afford a decent meal. This is something you have to think about—something you have ignored. And I will *not* hold myself back from helping them now. Sorry to disappoint you, like always." Jinhai sneered.

"Kings are not supposed to sit with the peasants on the streets!" Qianfan bellowed.

"You have simply forgotten what being a king means," Jinhai replied. "Maybe you should think about the sins that are holding you back, the sins that are affecting your good nature."

Qianfan boiled in rage. "How *dare* you speak to your father like that?"

Jinhai grinned, and then calmly uttered, "Pardon me, I have to go. I'm running late for the *food drive*."

He left the room, leaving Qianfan standing there alone with an army of guards that were gathered outside Jinhai's door. Jinhai knew that his father was powerless to stop him, and he *never* let him get on his nerves. Their encounters were entertaining for Jinhai, just as they were humiliating for Qianfan. Their exchanges were only words for now, but Jinhai knew that when he takes the throne, Qianfan would only make things difficult for him.

Jinhai quickly wolfed down his breakfast, then left with Xiaosheng for the main market down by the harbor—the hub for all the trading shops and where many of the homeless resided. When they arrived, there were already many residents carrying boxes full of clothes and food to donate, all willing to help out wherever they could. Jinhai wanted Xiaosheng to see how helping others had a ripple effect—how one person's small offering could give others a chance to pay it forward. Haitao and his father were there, too, but they were standing next to someone that Jinhai had never met—a beautiful woman.

"Jinhai!" Haitao shouted from a distance.

"Haitao, my friend!" Jinhai shouted back, and then they shook each other's hand. "Good to see you!"

"Always a pleasure to see you doing great things, my son," Lixin commented.

"It's all because of you," Jinhai assured him with a grin.

"Oh, I almost forgot—meet Fia. She just moved in next door. She's new to town, so we thought we'd bring her along and introduce her to the community." Haitao winked at Jinhai.

"Hi!" Fia cheerfully greeted.

She had a thin face with rosy cheeks, a fair

complexion, and her smile was accompanied by dimples on both her cheeks.

"Hi," Jinhai greeted back with a grin. But then he abruptly excused himself when someone called for him.

Jinhai was never into romance or attracting attention to himself. He knew he easily caught the eyes of many women around him, but he never gave them a second thought. He stayed away from anything heartfelt, and from afar, he seemed extremely unapproachable. His parents' relationship had affected him a great deal. They made him think that love between two people would always be temporary—a waste of time—so there's really no point in chasing it.

He had his boundaries set, and he never crossed them... until now. Fia. He couldn't stop thinking about her. Her beautiful smile, her bubbly personality. She brought him a certain sense of... comfort. She felt like pure light to him.

People all around him were preparing for the food drive. Wooden tables were set up on a red carpet that was spread along the pathway, containers full of food were brought in, and everyone was invited to take their places while the volunteers started to serve them.

Fia was one of those volunteers, and the way she committed to the cause caught Jinhai's attention. She approached people with a smile and asked them how they were doing in a welcoming tone. They complimented her, and she laughed before moving onto the next person, making them all feel at home. Jinhai caught himself looking for her many times when she disappeared from his sight, and then he'd tell himself to snap out of it.

"Don't do this to yourself. You will become *nothing* but a hopeless romantic."

Haitao and Jinhai worked together at the drive. They re-filled the food containers as soon as they were empty. There were more than two hundred people who had shown up, and after they were all fed, the leftovers would be packed and sent home with them.

"You seem distracted today," Haitao teased.

"Why would I be distracted?" Jinhai asked.

"You tell me!" Haitao laughed.

"What do you mean?"

"I've noticed that your attention is on... a certain someone."

"Well, maybe you should be noticing how you're spilling beans all over the floor," Jinhai replied with a sneer.

Haitao looked down at the beans that covered his shoes before laughing. "The beans have fallen, just like you."

Jinhai shook his head, speechless.

After serving the food, all the volunteers gathered around the food containers to pack the leftovers. They all sat down in a circle and quickly filled up the bags around them. Jinhai couldn't help but notice how Fia and Xiaosheng had gotten very close, almost like they were sisters.

A middle-aged woman from the circle spoke up as she filled a bag, "All these people are suffering because the kingdom is failing. How is this ever going to get better?"

The townspeople of Jinu felt comfortable voicing their concerns to Jinhai, despite him being a prince. Unlike his father, he listened, and he never judged them. But before he could answer, Fia chimed in.

"You know how when stars fall, we make a wish? But we don't see those stars as falling; we see them as a chance to pray for a miracle. Think about our situation in the same way. Sure, things aren't that great now, but I believe that if we want it enough, a miracle will soon happen."

"I never thought of it like that," the woman replied.

"What a wonderful comparison, Fia!" Lixin exclaimed.

"I agree!" Xiaosheng added and looked over at Jinhai, who remained silent.

The sun soon started to set, just as the volunteers were finishing up. The sky had turned dark blue, and as the light slowly dimmed, the wind grew stronger, and the waves of the ocean aggressively crashed into the shore.

CHAPTER
TWO

LIXIN INVITED THE GROUP BACK TO HIS HOME FOR SOME TEA, and Jinhai and Xiaosheng eagerly accepted. After all, they called that place their *home*, the one place they felt safe in ever since they were just children. And the only reason they stayed at the castle was because of Jiayi. As a servant to the royal couple, she was never allowed to leave.

When they walked inside, Haitao, Fia, and Xiaosheng went to sit by the fireplace. Jinhai lit the logs before heading into the kitchen to help Lixin with the tea. Ever since Jinhai was young, they'd always bonded that way.

"My father visited me today, wanted me to stop the food drive," Jinhai said.

"And you made the right decision," Lixin assured him.

"He's always trying to make me a version of him, always trying to kill my compassionate side," Jinhai let out in frustration. "I like that I can feel other emotions and understand what others are going through. It helps me understand them better, and I come up with better solutions when I can relate to people."

Lixin smiled with a sense of relief. "That is your strength, Jinhai. You will never be able to experience any other emotion fully if you don't also let yourself feel the negative ones. You are in touch with your emotional side, and it is a blessing. You don't have to be strong and follow what your father tells you. I am proud of who you have become." Lixin paused, picking up the tea that he had just poured into the wooden cups, and then continued, "You are going to make a fine leader one day."

Jinhai nodded, grabbed the plate with baked bread and sliced cakes off the counter, and followed Lixin back into the living room.

"My favorite!" Xiaosheng jumped up excitedly and grabbed a slice of cake.

"This is literally the best bread that I have ever had," Fia added. "I will certainly take some home."

"Me, too!" Xiaosheng approved.

"So, who's this prince that everyone keeps talking about today? The entire kingdom seems to like him, and they say he's their last hope," Fia then asked.

Xiaosheng looked at Jinhai, and they all soon realized that Fia had no idea that Xiaosheng and Jinhai were royalty—that *they* were the future of this kingdom.

"I'm curious myself," Haitao joked.

"What do you mean?" Fia chuckled. "You've never seen him?"

"Fia," Lixin grinned, "I believe you have not been properly introduced." He paused, and then pointed at Jinhai. "Meet Jinhai, the *prince* of Jinu."

Jinhai looked into her eyes and smiled.

"Oh...," Fia murmured, embarrassed.

"And meet Xiaosheng, the *princess* of Jinu," Lixin revealed.

"Hi!" Xiaosheng laughed.

"Why do you seem so disappointed?" Haitao asked.

"I'm not disappointed, just... surprised," Fia replied, and then continued in an apologetic tone, "I hope I didn't offend anyone. I didn't know."

Haitao laughed again, and then jokingly said, "You have, and now you're going to prison for life!"

"Haitao's just messing around. You didn't offend us. I prefer *not* to be treated like royalty anyway," Jinhai finally spoke.

Fia was still shocked that the cute boy she'd been hanging around all day, one who looked just like everyone else in town, was actually the prince of this kingdom, the one destined to save it from poverty and destruction. He's so... so... different, so kind. Suddenly, she found herself being drawn to him, but had to take a step back. "I should get going. It's getting late."

"Alright, don't forget the bread!" Haitao reminded her.

"Oh, yes." Fia beamed, and Lixin handed her a box filled with some. "Thank you."

"It was nice meeting you. See you soon!" Xiaosheng waved.

"See you soon," Fia replied.

She didn't say anything to Jinhai, but their eyes met before she walked out of the door.

"I really like her," Xiaosheng sang.

"Seems like you're not the only one," Haitao added.

"Who are we talking about?" Jinhai asked.

"Oh, don't act naïve," Haitao teased.

"Wait... Jinhai?" Xiaosheng chuckled.

"Xiaosheng, have you ever seen your brother this quiet?" Haitao asked.

Xiaosheng paused, and then shook her head. "No, I haven't." She shot her gaze over at her brother. "You like her!"

Jinhai muttered, "I just met her." He shook his head. "I don't even know her."

"You're not denying it, though," Haitao teased again.

"I am not agreeing, either," Jinhai insisted.

"Alright, alright!" Xiaosheng laughed.

"She's a strong one. Fia's parents died when she was very young. She spent the majority of her childhood at an orphanage that wasn't safe for anyone. She only recently moved here because she wanted to start fresh, to find a new home. Even now, she's living alone, and she works at the flower shop to support herself. She mentioned that when she's financially stable enough, she'll dedicate her life to helping orphans who can't help themselves, so they don't have to go through what she went through," Haitao explained.

"What an inspiration!" Xiaosheng exclaimed.

"Yeah," Jinhai murmured.

Later that night, Jinhai and Xiaosheng walked back to the castle, where they found Jiayi cooking up something delicious. Xiaosheng rushed over to hug her.

"How was your day?" Jiayi asked as they sat down for dinner.

Xiaosheng told her everything, including how they'd met a woman who was *perfect* for Jinhai. "She's pretty. She's kind. She's perfect!"

"You're blushing, Jinhai, something I've never seen you do," Jiayi pointed out. "There seems to be a bit of truth in what Xiaosheng is saying."

"There's nothing going on. We *did* just meet," Jinhai assured them.

"Only time will tell." Jiayi nodded.

Jinhai went into his room after dinner and closed

the door behind him. His room was huge, with different types of swords hanging on the walls and painted portraits of martyrs whom he admired. The sheets on his bed were made of blue silk, and the walls were white but covered with velvet curtains.

It had been a long day, and while he was tired, he couldn't fall asleep. He just couldn't get Fia out of his mind.

"How could someone have gone through so much but still have such a positive outlook on life? I don't understand."

Jinhai woke up the next morning to the sound of roaring thunder. He rolled out of bed and looked out the window. The wind was strong and getting stronger by the second, the streets were emptier than usual, and the sky was covered in dark gray clouds that looked menacing and threatening.

He could see the harbor from his window. The waves in the ocean were unsettling, hitting the rocks by the shore with force, and ships were swinging from side to side. Jinhai had never seen the weather this bad before, and he was worried about his people, especially the ones without shelter.

However, it wasn't raining yet. He still had time to get everyone safely inside somewhere before it began to pour. He rushed over to his closet to get dressed, choosing a traditional attire over the old rags that he usually wore. He needed to feel powerful in order to complete this morning's mission.

As he secured his kingdom's broach onto his lapel, he looked in the mirror and grinned at his reflection.

"There's no mistaking that I'm a prince now."

Suddenly, he heard a knock on his door, and it swung open to Qianfan walking in.

"Spying on me, Father?" Jinhai asked, staring at his father's reflection in the glass.

"Trust me, I wouldn't be here if I didn't have to be," Qianfan said in a stern voice before asking, "Have you discovered your power yet?"

Jinhai knew about the power that had been bestowed upon him and the stories of the magical stone, but he had never experienced anything magical in his life. He didn't even know where to begin.

"I have not," Jinhai replied.

"Always a disappointment," Qianfan huffed. "I knew you were weak the day you were born. Your chances of becoming king are dwindling by the minute."

Jinhai remained silent and let patience take over his mind with a deep breath. He was using everything he had to not explode at his father.

"What a wimp," Qianfan taunted and dramatically left the room, slamming the door shut behind him.

Jinhai was worried—not because of what Qianfan had said, but because he felt incomplete without his power. If he was blessed with one, then why was it taking so long to come to fruition?

He quickly pushed the thought out of his head and joined Jiayi and Xiaosheng for breakfast.

"The weather outside is so scary! Have you seen it? It feels like the night has eaten the sun." Xiaosheng gestured toward the window while sipping her tea.

"Yes, stay indoors today, Xiaosheng. You, too, Jiayi. Please stay with Xiaosheng," Jinhai muttered as he walked in.

"What about you? Where are *you* headed?" Jiayi asked a bit sarcastically.

"The weather is bad... and only getting worse by the minute. Our less fortunate brothers and sisters are sleeping by the harbor; they are going to need shelter. I have to make sure that they are taken care of. I'll be fine. Do not worry," Jinhai assured.

"Can someone else not do it? It's not safe out there. The wind is angry, and I can sense a vicious storm brewing."

"No. This is our kingdom, our people. We *have* to take care of them; we *have* to be there for them." He gently touched Jiayi on the hand and whispered, "I promise to come right back once my duties are done." He stood up hugged them both before grabbing his belongings and walking out to his carriage.

When he reached the harbor, there were crowds of people running around in a panic. One of the ships had crashed onto the land, damaging several homes and injuring many with no help in sight. The waves of the ocean were growing higher and higher with every push, and the ships that were still standing were starting to lose control against the strong currents. A crowd had gathered around the site of the crash—men, women, and children all desperate to save those trapped beneath it.

"We need to get everyone back into their homes or into one of our military-grade shelters! Now!" Jinhai shouted over to his guards.

As he uttered his last words, one of the waves began to levitate the largest ship over the ocean. Jinhai saw the scene unfold before him in horror and looked over at the crowd that stood in front of it.

If this falls, it will be a bloodbath, a great tragedy. I cannot have this on my conscience.

He felt shivers rush through his body, but he knew he needed to do what he came out here to do—protect the people. He rushed over to the crowd and began pushing them aside, flailing his arms in every direction in an attempt to clear the path.

"Move out of the way!" he screamed as he glanced over at the ocean and saw the wave push the ship toward the harbor with a mighty force. "No!" he shouted as he moved both of his hands toward the ocean and squeezed his eyes shut.

His heart was pounding in his chest, and he felt a sinking feeling in his stomach. He clenched his fists in anticipation for the loud crash and screaming cries that would soon lead to death. He waited for all of it.

But it never came.

Silence.

No screams.

What happened? A miracle?

Jinhai slowly crept his eyes open, still expecting to see a massacre before him, but what he saw was much... stranger.

His hands were still lifted in the air, toward the ocean, and the deadly wave appeared as if it were frozen. The people all looked at Jinhai in shock, then they started cheering for him. Not knowing what to do next, Jinhai slowly brought his hands back down, and to his surprise, the water followed, and the mighty waves merged back into the water.

He fell onto his knees with his hands over his head. He could only feel gratitude—the scene had been witnessed by the people of his kingdom who would now think of him as a hero. Fia, Haitao, and Lixin, who were all there to help the homeless move into shelters, had also witnessed his heroic act.

Suddenly, a bright light flashed from the clouds as a streak of lightning struck the ocean nearby, and a loud clap of thunder boomed as the wind grew stronger again.

"Everyone needs to leave!" Jinhai yelled as it began to rain heavily, and the crowd started to disperse.

"You, too. I'll stay behind to make sure everyone's gone." Jinhai turned toward Haitao and Fia.

"No, we're not leaving you," Fia fought back.

"Agree. We will stay and help."

"Where's Lixin?" Jinhai asked.

"At the shelter. He took a bunch of people with him."

After hours of thoroughly searching the harbor, making sure no child was stuck under a rock and no father was lost trying to find his way, they all walked toward the shelter. The rain was getting heavier and heavier as time passed, and they were soaking wet by the time they arrived.

Jinhai was greeted with applauses of encouragement and chants of appreciation as he walked inside. Family after family came up to him, thanking him for everything that he did. The prince bowed his head in respect every time someone shook his hand, and Fia admired him from afar. The affection. The determination. The respect. Something that she had never seen before.

And the shelter itself, a former military unit for the storage of firearms and armor, was massive and stocked with everything they'd need for the night. There were enough warm meals to go around, hot tea to cool down those coming down with an illness, and the injured were quickly treated. The people of Jinu residing there all gathered around the fireplace, reminiscing their experiences of the prince's magnificent miracle.

"A miracle. It truly *is* a miracle," Jinhai repeated over and over to himself as he changed into garments that were less damp. "Almost too good to be a miracle—"

"You finally figured it out," Lixin interrupted from around the corner, causing Jinhai to slightly hop.

"The Universe figured it out for me."

"*You* did this, all on your own, Jinhai. Have some faith in yourself." Lixin smiled. "Look around you. All these people are safe for another day because of *you*, because *you* woke up this morning and decided to risk your own life for them. You could've stayed home, much like your father did, but you didn't. That's the difference between a great leader and a coward."

Jinhai gave him a shy grin.

"And all it took was a little bit of emotion," Lixin continued.

"What do you mean?" Jinhai asked.

"Legend has it, the powers that your family has only reveal themselves through pure emotions. You must've been holding back all these years, and when you allowed yourself to be scared and concerned over the safety of the people back at the harbor, that's when your power came to life."

Jinhai's shy grin turned into a full smile. He turned around and looked for Fia in the crowd, where he saw her wrap a tiny four-year-old child in a blanket.

"You will catch a cold." He heard her faint voice from a distance.

How can you fall for someone you barely know? he asked himself.

"It's all because of her," he caught himself saying out loud.

"Because of who?" Lixin asked, and then noticed Jinhai blush. "Are you hiding something from me? You are, aren't you?"

Jinhai chuckled. "I think I have feelings for Fia. I

can't stop thinking about her. I can't stop dreaming about her beautiful face. I believe that it's because of her that I am able to become emotionally vulnerable. I feel like she is my soulmate."

"You know, when my wife died, I couldn't believe it. For months, I was a wreck because I felt incomplete without her, like someone had taken away a piece of my heart. Losing her made me realize how much I took her for granted, her smile, her laughter, even her words. Even my own name sounded different after she was gone. But at the same time, it made me want to cherish the one thing that I had left of her even more, my son. So, I pieced myself together, put on a brave face, and promised her that no matter what, I will take care of our child. I will live for the both of us." Lixin sighed before continuing. "Treasure the way that you're feeling now... because you never know when you'll feel the same way again. Tell her how you really feel. Don't take her for granted like I did."

THREE

THE SHELTER SOON CALMED, AND SILENCE TOOK OVER AS THE night went on. The children had stopped running around, and everyone was growing sleepy after their large dinner of boiled white rice and garlic-seasoned chicken.

"Prince Jinhai, we have informed Xiaosheng and Jiayi about your safety, and that you will be staying here for the night," one of the guards told Jinhai.

"Thank you," Jinhai replied.

After the guards left, the prince took a deep breath. "I hope they weren't too worried. Jiayi *did* have a hunch that something bad was going to happen. She must be under great levels of stress. I am ashamed of myself for having caused that."

Haitao had fallen asleep, and Lixin was silently sipping his fourth cup of tea.

"It's not your fault," Fia comforted him. "You were exactly where you were meant to be. Right place at the right time. You have saved so many lives today. Jiayi is only going to be proud of you." She smiled. "Imagine how many families you have saved from being broken, how many children you have protected, Prince Jinhai."

"You don't have to call me that. You can just call me by my name. You are just like Haitao to me, a friend. Thank you for sticking around and helping out."

Before Fia could say another word, Lixin chimed in.

"Goodnight, both of you. I'm off to sleep. I'll see you all in the morning."

"Goodnight," Jinhai whispered.

"Sleep well," Fia wished to Lixin as he walked off.

For the first time since they met, Jinhai and Fia were finally alone, sitting in front of each other by the fireplace. Fia's face was glowing as the orange light of the fire met her face, and it made her smile even warmer, which softened Jinhai's heart.

"Aren't you tired? It's been a long day," Jinhai asked.

"No." Fia shook her head with her eyes glued to the

flames of the fire. "This is nothing compared to what I'm used to."

"I can believe that. Haitao mentioned your past struggles. Your resilience is admirable."

Fia blushed. "Thank you."

"Can I ask you a question?"

"Of course," Fia responded.

"You've been through so much and have faced so many injustices. I'm sure living without parents and at an orphanage is *not* easy. But you still have this calmness in your soul, this willingness to still help others even when no one helped you. How?"

As Fia listened, she realized that Jinhai *had* been thinking about her, and her heart tingled slightly. "There are so many things in our lives that we cannot control... except for our reactions to those things. I just don't see a point in letting the bad destroy me when there's nothing that I can do to stop it from happening." Fia paused, then continued, "There's always a silver lining if I look hard enough."

"Every time I interact with you, you leave me speechless. Your point of view is so different from that of others. It's extremely uplifting, even in the darkest of days," Jinhai muttered in a low voice.

"I leave you speechless?" Fia asked as she laughed.

"Yes, you do. I'm not usually someone who gets quiet around people, but around you, I... you make me nervous."

"Nervous? Around me? I'm the one who should be

nervous around you! You're a prince! And you're magical!"

"B...," Jinhai stuttered, "because I... because I like you."

"What are saying, Jinhai?" Fia asked.

"I'm saying that I am drawn to you, that you complete me. You are the reason I was able to save lives today. Before today, I had no control over my power. I was even growing distraught because I thought I didn't have any. It wasn't until I met you and started becoming emotionally vulnerable did it finally unleash. You were the key that I needed." He looked down at his feet and shuffled. "I understand if you do not feel the same way. Lixin made me realize today that life is too short to hold in my feelings any longer. I just needed you to know. I want you by my side day after day."

"Truth is, Jinhai, I sort of felt the same way, but you're a prince! How could an orphan girl like me even have a chance? You could have anyone you want in this entire kingdom... plus more! I'm outnumbered!" Her eyes started to fill with tears as she spoke.

"Hey, why are you crying? This is great news!" Jinhai tried to console her, wiping away her tears.

"But it's never going to work. One day, you will become King. And you are destined to marry a princess. I don't even have a family!"

"So? Those things don't matter to me. The throne doesn't matter to me. I only care about the people around me. Xiaosheng loves you, Haitao and Lixin praise you, and Jiayi will be over the moon to meet you, I promise. *You* matter to me, not some stupid crown or the label of royalty." Jinhai held onto her hands as Fia shifted herself closer to him and rested her head on his arm.

"I should go to sleep. It's getting late," Fia whispered.

"See you tomorrow?" Jinhai asked.

"Of course." Fia smiled. "Goodnight."

Jinhai was shocked by what he had just done. That was the most spontaneous he'd ever been his entire life! And he didn't fall flat on his face. He was grinning from ear to ear. No more fighting with himself and wishing for some girl in the corner of his room. She liked him back! He vowed to himself that he'd protect her and keep her close from now on.

Fia, on the other hand, was overwhelmed, but she wasn't complaining. A prince had just told her that he wanted her! Her whole life, all she ever wanted was to be wanted, and what she got was way better than she'd expected. Jinhai brought out the best version of her. She felt like herself around him—she smiled a little brighter, laughed a little louder. He completed her, just like she completed him. She just hoped that things would work out between them, and that the Universe wouldn't test her like it always did.

It was a new day, both literally and metaphorically. The sun shone in the blue sky with hints of white clouds, and the birds were singing with joy. The storm had passed, but a lot changed for both the kingdom and for Jinhai.

He woke up to the smell of tofu and realized that Lixin was making breakfast. He quickly got up and looked around—everyone had gone back to their homes. Only Haitao, Lixin, and Fia were left inside the shelter, waiting for Jinhai to wake up so they could all eat.

"Prince Sleepyhead is finally awake," Haitao teased.

"Why didn't anyone wake me?" Jinhai asked in a tired voice.

"You seemed like you were enjoying your rest. We didn't want to disturb you," Fia replied and gave him a flirtatious wink. Jinhai blushed.

"Breakfast is served," Lixin interrupted the three and placed an enormous pot of steaming hot tofu in front of them.

After a heavy breakfast, Lixin and Fia walked back to their village while Haitao stayed behind with Jinhai for a little longer.

"So?" Haitao asked as they walked out of the shelter and into the blazing sun.

"So?" Jinhai repeated.

"You have fallen for her pretty face, haven't you?" Haitao teased.

"The human face does not reflect the beauty that

the soul within holds," Jinhai responded. This was his way of teasing Haitao back; he knew how much he hated poetic replies.

"Oh, stop with this nonsense," Haitao said with a sneer.

"Fine, fine. Yes, I have fallen for her pretty face!" Jinhai laughed. "Xiaosheng is definitely going to be happy when she hears this."

"I never thought this day would come. Jinhai, the boy who once swore to never become emotionally attached to anyone, has fallen in love."

"Yeah, well, people can change... I should probably get going. Jiayi must be worried sick." Jinhai waved farewell to his friend and walked off in the opposite direction.

Jinhai found Jiayi and his sister both waiting for him in his room when he reached the castle.

"Morning," Jinhai mumbled in a tired tone.

"Thank goodness! You're okay!" Xiaosheng screamed in relief and ran over to hug him tight.

"I am *so* proud of you. I've heard many stories about your bravery at the harbor," Jiayi praised with a smile and prideful eyes. Her words made him realize how Fia was right—Jiayi *was* the first to praise him.

"Thank you." Jinhai bowed his head.

"And I've heard about your newfound power. It's so cool that you can control water!" Xiaosheng exclaimed in excitement and hugged him again.

"Now you'll have to think twice before playing anymore pranks on me... unless you want to drown," her brother taunted while Xiaosheng gave him a playful push. Then his tone grew more serious. "And... I told Fia how I am attracted to her, and how I want to be with her."

"What did she say? Did she reject you?" Xiaosheng asked. She was not surprised at all by his confession.

"She said..." Jinhai stopped.

"Well, tell us!" Jiayi urged.

"She said she likes me, too." Jinhai grinned.

"I can't believe this!" Xiaosheng screamed and jumped up and down.

"I was hoping I could bring her over for dinner tonight... if that's okay with you, Jiayi," Jinhai requested.

"I don't see why not!" Jiayi agreed.

"But keep it low-key. I don't want anyone knowing about this just yet. You know how word travels fast around here."

"My lips are sealed," Jiayi assured the prince.

About an hour later, Jinhai took a quick bath and got ready. He was going to go down to the harbor and invite Fia over for dinner. He threw on a royal blue qipao and pinned on a brooch that had a bird engraved onto it, symbolizing peace and harmony. He then summoned his carriage, gathered his guards, and left for the harbor.

The conditions at the harbor were bad, really bad. What used to be the pride and joy of Jinu was now heavily damaged and falling apart. He walked around and inspected every inch of his surroundings, giving orders to his guards on suggestions that he had to fix up the place and quickly.

Suddenly, someone tapped him on the shoulder. Jinhai quickly spun around, expecting to see Fia, but instead, he saw an elderly woman standing behind him. She was quite petite and had silver hair. Her face was covered with wrinkles, and she limped while leaning on her wooden stick for balance.

"Yes?" Jinhai politely answered the tap.

"Thank you," the old woman whispered. "You saved my son yesterday. If you hadn't been there, I would be mourning his loss today." She bowed respectfully. "I wish for you to overtake your father and rule the land. You deserve to seize the throne."

Jinhai never really knew what to say whenever someone complimented him. Instead, he simply bowed back and accepted her gratitude.

"If you had been born sooner, your sisters may not have suffered the fate that they had," the woman continued.

Jinhai's heart briefly stopped, and his stomach dropped.

"What do you mean?" he asked.

"You do not know? Your older sisters, Xiuying and Xiaofan. They were both abandoned because your father so desperately wanted a son. Xiuying's nanny was my sister, Mei, and your father sentenced her to life in prison."

Jinhai could not believe his ears. How was this the first time he was hearing about all this?

"Are they... are they... alive? Do you know what happened to them?" Jinhai asked frantically. His entire life, he thought he only had one sister, Xiaosheng.

"I know as much as you do. My child, it is almost as if they had been forgotten. Not many people in the kingdom know about them. I only know bits and pieces of what had happened because my sister witnessed everything with her own two eyes." The woman then added, "Everyone who knew about your sisters were either imprisoned or killed by your father."

Jinhai stood silent, trying to process everything that he had just heard within the span of five minutes. "There must be *someone* still around who knows what *actually* happened to them! Think, who else knows?"

The old woman hesitated for a moment, but then she revealed, "You have to meet Huiqing. He was Chief of the Military at the time and imprisoned with Mei as an accomplice. He might know something that nobody else does."

"Where? Where can I find him?"

"Locked inside a prison cell deep within the castle. You could try, but he might already be dead," she replied.

Jinhai nodded his head. "Thank you for telling me this."

"Do not let this information go to waste, my child. You are the only one who can save your sisters."

As the woman strolled away, Jinhai stared out into the ocean, where the waves were crashing against the shore. "My father is an evil man. There is no denying that he is capable of something like this. I have to get to the bottom of this."

The guards were all given orders to tend to the harbor while Jinhai had more important things to worry about. Fia. With the words of the woman and his father's atrocious actions still in his mind, he hopped inside his carriage and rode away.

FOUR

AFTER A SHORT RIDE, JINHAI REACHED HIS DESTINATION AND walked down the street toward Fia's shop. He stood there for a minute and watched her put together a bouquet of flowers, placing each stem carefully in its place. Her hair was tied with a ribbon that matched the robe she wore, and he admired how she always made sure her colors matched. There was just something about her that gave him peace amidst all the chaos around him.

After a few more minutes, he walked in. He had

spent much too long staring at her through the window that it was starting to get weird.

Fia greeted the prince with a cheerful tone when she saw him. "Hi! What are you doing here?"

"I had some things to take care of in town and thought I'd pop in to see you."

"Really?"

"No," Jinhai admitted.

"Then?" Fia chuckled as she asked.

"I came here to invite you over for dinner tonight. I want you to meet Jiayi. She's been a mother to me my entire life when my birth mother didn't want me."

"Well, if you put it like that, how can I possibly refuse?" Fia smirked sarcastically.

"I can have a carriage come by later to pick you up," Jinhai offered.

"No, no. It's fine. I'm a grown woman. I'm sure I can find my way there. Besides, it's not like I can see it from here or anything." Fia pointed over to her left. And when Jinhai looked over, he saw one of the large castle towers looming over the village.

"Fair point," he acknowledged, "but let me send one anyway. It'll be my way of showing my appreciation for all that you do."

"If you insist." She grinned, though there was still hesitation in her voice.

When Jinhai left to head back to the harbor, Fia still felt a pang of guilt. The differences between her and Jinhai were infinite. They weren't even part of the same social circle! He came from wealth and gold while she came from poverty and destitute. How was she ever going to stand a chance with him without everyone around her mocking her and judging her? She would forever be labeled a *gold digger*, or even worse, a *prostitute*.

On the other hand, she knew that Jinhai didn't see her in that way at all, and she knew she couldn't let the sneers of others cut in between them. Their relationship was between the two of them, not the world around them.

After making sure that everything was in order at the harbor, Jinhai went back to the castle with just one intention—to visit Huiqing and find out the truth. Part of him prayed that the old woman was just delusional and spewing nonsense, but the other part of him didn't expect anything less from his parents.

It was already late in the afternoon when he got back. He slowly made his way down the halls, ones that he wasn't very familiar with as he was usually confined to his room, and headed down the dark staircase into the abandoned hall of the basement. There were two guards protecting the only door, surrounded by lit oil lamps and the freezing cold air.

"No one is allowed inside," one of the guards stated firmly.

"I believe you are forgetting who I am. I may just be a prince right now, but soon, this will be *my* kingdom. Your actions now will surely determine your fate in Jinu," Jinhai warned them with a strong yet soothing tone.

"Yes, your highness," the guard replied and opened the door of iron rods, sealed with chains and locks.

Jinhai knew that the door wasn't to be opened without the king's permission, and so he assured the guards that this would stay between them as he stepped inside. He walked into a small alley that had tiny rooms on both sides with no windows. They were also covered with iron rods, chained and locked in the same manner as the front door.

He shivered as he walked past three empty cells, and then three more that housed people who were on the verge of dying. He could see that the lack of food, water, sunlight, and hygienic facilities had made it challenging for them all to survive.

"This is torture," he heard himself mutter.

It was so dark that it felt like it was past midnight. There were rats crawling all over the floor and water coming out of the broken pipes.

"How? How is this justice? I get to sit upstairs on my golden throne while these people down here are forced to eat their own excrements."

Jinhai walked to the end of the alley, finding two more cells that faced each other. One of them was empty with nothing but a tiny window inside, while the other housed a very ancient man with a long beard and a pale face. He was sitting up, staring out the tiny window, so focused on the light coming in that he didn't realize that someone had approached him.

"Huiqing?" Jinhai spoke softly.

The man slowly glanced up at him, frightened.

No one had come to see him in years, left alone to relive his terrifying memories.

"I have not heard my name in ages," the man whispered in a strong voice.

Jinhai was shocked when he heard the man's voice. For someone who seemed so weak, his voice didn't match his appearance at all.

"Who is here to see me?" Huiqing asked.

"Jinhai," Jinhai replied.

Huiqing paused. "The awaited Prince of Jinu? I have heard good things about you. I have heard that you are quite the opposite of your father. What is someone so high and mighty like yourself doing down here in the cells?"

The question haunted Jinhai. Huiqing was here, imprisoned, and the possibility of the tale being true was elevated. Did he even have the courage to learn the truth?

"Seems like you're a little lost, Little One," Huiqing continued.

Jinhai took a deep breath and sat down beside the iron rods that separated him from Huiqing. "The search for peace—for truth—brings me here to you, Huiqing. I have been told a tale by someone who claimed to be Mei's sister," Jinhai said, looking down at his hands.

"You seem anxious, Little One, and rightfully so. It is not just a tale that you have been told, but it's the truth that, I assume, has been hidden from you for decades. It is what has happened before you. It is what people have experienced for only showing kindness, for only wanting love. It is the injustice that took our lives away," Huiqing explained almost poetically. His voice was firm but painful that it sent shivers down Jinhai's spine.

"Xiuying was born first, the eldest. Your mother adored her, but your father so desperately wanted a son instead. So, they gave her to Mei. Your parents abandoned her, and they announced to the kingdom that Xiuying had died at birth. But shortly after, the queen—your mother—started to feel resentment toward Mei for being Xiuying's first priority. Because of all the trauma, Xiuying attempted to take her own life one night. Luckily, she survived. Mei, with her motherly instincts, went against the queen and king, fought for Xiuying's rights and the love that she needed, but in return, she was forced to spend the rest of her life here." He pointed toward the empty cell in front of his, the one with the tiny window.

"I was ordered to drop Xiuying off on a deserted island to die so that your parents could be free of their mistake, but I couldn't do that to her. Instead, I left her in the care of some amazing village people whom I knew would care for her well. She was wronged by everyone here, and life was extremely difficult for her, being sent away by her own blood mother, after all. However, when I came back, your father soon found out what I had done and sentenced me to spend the rest of my life down here."

Jinhai stayed silent. He didn't know what to say.

He hated the way that his father had treated him, but to force someone who had once been loyal to him to die of starvation was much worse than he could've imagined. Qianfan. He just wasn't human!

"I'm so sorry," Jinhai apologized on his father's behalf. "I didn't know about any of this."

"I loved her. Mei. We spent years and years together down here. She continued to praise Xiuying until the day she died and told herself that it was all worth it. Unfortunately, the torture that she underwent would be fatal for anyone. They forced her to stand on swords for hours, starved her for days at a time, and mercilessly whipped her until she admitted that she never loved your sister—which she'd never do. She was beaten to death simply because your mother resented her. Your mother constantly blamed Mei for Xiuying's hatred for the queen. Always blaming everyone but herself and her own damn husband."

Huiqing broke into tears and started to cry. Jinhai's eyes turned red with rage, remorse, and regret, tears rolling down from them. His heart had become too heavy. He could feel himself drowning in the pit of despair. He was so oblivious, so unaware... that his parents were the human version of the Devil. With no words to describe the sorrow, no will to speak for the injustices that his father had done, the lives he had destroyed, Jinhai thought it couldn't get any worse... but then Huiqing continued.

"Xiaofan was born next. Your father played his

cards with this one. At first, Xiaofan was accepted, welcomed, and celebrated. Your mother was at ease with the fact that Qianfan had accepted a girl, but to him, Xiaofan was only a pawn, a gateway to finally bearing a son. And when you were born, everything changed. Now that the king finally got what he wanted, he no longer saw a need to keep Xiaofan around. So, he sent her away to an abandoned orphanage in the middle of a destitute town known for its darkness and horrendous crimes. And of course, the queen stayed silent throughout all this, as usual. She'd never go against her husband." Huiqing paused for a moment to swallow his tears. "Oh, and don't even get me started on your evil grandmother. She was the worst of them all when it came to Xiuying."

Qiang had always been nothing but a saint to Jinhai, the sweet grandmother who took care of him and fed him. He couldn't imagine someone like her ever being capable of anything else.

"Do you know where they are? Are my sisters still alive?" Jinhai nervously asked.

"Qiang was supposed to meet them. They are alive, and they live together, but that is all I know. Your grandmother mentioned this when she last visited me, and right after, she hopped on a boat to go see them," Huiqing replied.

Jinhai remembered the voyage that his grand-mother took just before she died. It took her over two weeks to come back, and Jinhai remembered the argu-ment that Qiang had with his father the night she died. Jinhai was shaken to know how much clearer everything was. It all made sense now.

"I am sorry about your grandmother's passing. My condolences... but something inside me tells me that it was not a coincidence," Huiqing spoke.

"What do you mean?"

Ignoring Jinhai's question, Huiqing continued, "I don't know what happened after or what happened at the voyage, but there is a way for you to find out. Your grandmother always carried a journal. Every time she came down here, she would write down all our conversations. For sentimental reasons? Maybe. But I think it's to catch anything I say that could lead to my impending death. If you find it, I'm sure you might be able to find some answers."

"Yes, yes!" Jinhai jumped up as he remembered. "She *did* take her journal with her, and she *did* bring it back. It must be in her room somewhere. Thank you, Huiqing, for everything." Jinhai paused. His voice was shaky as he stood up, holding onto the iron rods with his sweaty palms. "You took care of my sister when my parents did not. You protected her when my parents had left her to die, and I will never forget that. I am in your debt with all that you have done, and I promise that I will find a way to get you and everyone who have faced injustices at the hands of my father out of here. Until then, I will make sure that you have everything you need to live comfortably."

"I wish to see the sun one day and the crown on your head. But now, you must leave. It's getting late, and if your father catches you, he'll lock you down here, too," Huiqing replied. "And remember, don't let your father know that you are aware of his wrongdoings. Use this as your weapon. Don't let it become your weakness."

CHAPTER
FIVE

THE SUN HAD GONE DOWN, AND DARKNESS HAD TAKEN OVER with stars shimmering within the abyss. Jinhai had completely forgotten about dinner, and the fact that he had invited Fia over to meet Jiayi.

He sprinted out of the prison chambers and straight into Qiang's room... which he found bolted with thick metal chains. But he was tenacious, and he was *not* going to just give up. He needed to learn the rest of the story, and the anger that he held for his father was increasing with every second of anticipation. All he could think about was getting revenge—he was *not* going to let his dictator of a father get away with all that he had done. Jinhai was determined to take the throne and crown away from him, everything that had turned him into the egotistical and prideful snake that he was.

OVER ON THE OTHER SIDE OF TOWN, FIA HAD SPENT HER entire evening debating over what she was going to wear, how was she going to style her hair, and what she was going to say to one of the most important people in the prince's life. She was nervous, timid, but she was also super excited that something as amazing as dinner at the castle was actually happening to her.

But a big part of her missed her friends. If they were here now, they would've helped her with choosing the perfect outfit, and also tell her that she was being silly for doubting herself. Especially Xiaofan. She always liked to tease her. If only they could've all stayed together... But Xiaofan was with her sister now at a much better place than the orphanage, and she was sure the other girls also found a safe place to stay. *Anything* was better than that wretched town.

The overwhelming thoughts were eating her alive, and the sun had already set. She made herself a cup of oolong tea to calm her nerves, and then threw on the outfit that she had chosen. She finally decided on a traditional red qipao that covered her feet, and to finish the look, she clipped on her favorite necklace that had a tiny bird at the very center. She then walked over to her mirror and brushed a hint of pink across her cheeks and lined her lips with the darkest red gloss that she had.

When she finally stepped back, she looked different. She *felt* different. But she felt beautiful, and hopefully, that was enough to impress the prince. As she glanced outside the window, the color of the sky had shifted from a dark blue to a midnight black, but the stars deep within it continued to twinkle. She looked at them, and a smile grew on her face.

"This is really happening," she whispered to herself and took a deep breath. "For the first time since forever, I am finally getting what I've wished for."

She took in another breath and walked away from her window, eagerly waiting for the carriage to arrive as she sipped on her tea again. Within the next few minutes, she heard the sound of a bell outside. Her carriage had arrived.

"You look absolutely divine!" Xiaosheng blushed and complimented Fia as soon as she stepped inside the carriage.

"So do you!" Fia complimented back, and then they started catching up on each other's lives since they had last seen each other.

Jinhai was trying everything he could think of to break the lock on Qiang's door, but the more he tried, the more he was failing. He needed to get in, and he wondered why the room was even locked in the first place. What the hell was his father trying to hide?

There was an old willow tree just outside of Qiang's room, with thick branches that extended to her window. As a child, Jinhai used to climb across them and scare his grandmother, but he stopped after the day that Qianfan caught him and scolded him for disgracing the family name. That very memory flashed in his mind as he rushed toward it out in the garden.

It wasn't very dark outside, but it was just dark enough where no one would notice a grown man climbing up a tree. At the very least, he had to try. It was his only chance of getting inside the room. He tipped himself over onto his toes and hoisted himself up the trunk, frantically grabbing every part of it to keep himself from tumbling back down.

This was so much easier when I was a child.

When he finally made his way up, he carefully shifted his weight across one of the branches and toward Qiang's window. Luckily for him, it was unlocked! He grasped onto the ledge and jumped inside. Everything in her room was scattered haphazardly... as if someone had recently been in here, as if someone had been searching for something but failed to find whatever it was.

Jinhai lit a small candle and started to look around.

He searched all the wooden boxes, her rustic shelf of books, and even her closet, but he couldn't find her journal anywhere.

"Come on, please, I really need this," he whispered to himself in distress and sat down beside her bed. He tilted his head down with his hands wrapped around his knees.

"What am I going to do?" he asked himself as his eyes wandered across the floor, when suddenly, he saw a crack in between two floorboards.

"The secret box?" he whispered. "The secret box!"

The secret box was the hidden compartment beneath the floorboards of Qiang's room, where he used to hide his valuables from Xiaosheng. Oh, she was such a messy child, drawing all over everything she came across and smashing whatever would break against the ground. Jinhai thought it was a miracle the day he found this crack, a true refuge for all his special belongings.

"It's the secret box!" he repeated and rushed to open the crack.

THE CARRIAGE ARRIVED AT THE CASTLE, AND XIAOSHENG held onto Fia's hand as they both stepped out. This was Fia's first time ever seeing the luxurious sight around her, and she was even being treated as a royal as the guards that lined the staircase all bowed to her as she walked up the steps. The staircase was huge, and the wall was covered with wooden carvings and paintings. That, plus the marble floor and intricate statues, all made her feel very small, but she was excited to see what else was in store.

"This is my room, and right next door is Jinhai's room." Xiaosheng pointed from room to room before ending her finger toward the largest one in the hallway. "And this right here is where we're having dinner tonight. Come on!"

The dining room was simple yet still elegant. A long but short wooden table sat in the center of the room, and the floor was covered with a handwoven carpet that made Fia feel like she was walking on a cloud. The walls were decorated with oil paintings of what seemed to be childhood portraits of Jinhai and Xiaosheng. And a delicious aroma of chicken broth and fresh herbs filled the entire room. It was enough to make Fia's stomach rumble.

"I hope you're hungry!" Xiaosheng smiled beside her. "Jiayi makes the BEST noodle soup!"

"You must be Fia!" Jiayi sang as she walked in to greet them. "It's so nice to finally meet you! Jinhai has been singing your praises nonstop."

"I've heard a lot about you, too," Fia replied and bowed, to which Jiayi waved a hand to tell her that it was unnecessary.

"Where is Jinhai?" Jiayi asked Xiaosheng.

"I haven't seen him all day." Xiaosheng shrugged,

reaching across the table to help herself to a warm custard bun. "And he's not usually late for dinner, either."

"Hm, you're right. That's not like him at all," Jiayi wondered out loud. "I wonder where he could be."

CHAPTER
SIX

JINHAI LEANED OVER TO OPEN UP THE CRACK, HOPING TO FIND a childhood memorabilia inside. Instead, he found something much, much better. His grandmother's journal! She must've wanted whatever she wrote inside to stay a secret. And this intrigued Jinhai.

When he opened up to the first page, he saw his name.

Dearest Jinhai,

The blessed son who came into this family during the darkest of times. Your heart is pure like the water that the sea holds, and your soul radiates sunshine that represents the golden light within you. I have sinned my whole life, and I shall always regret it. Do not become like your father. It is too late for him. Rise, and be the king that Jinu needs.

Read my journal with your heart. With every written word inside, you'll learn about a terrible past that's awaiting your rectitude.

I will always love you.

Grandma

Jinhai's eyes watered, and he turned the page. Inside, were all her conversations with Huiqing, tons of details about his torture tales that he didn't disclose down in the dungeon. But it's never easy talking about something traumatic.

Apparently, Huiqing was branded a spy in the kingdom—a traitor—and was blamed for things that he never did. Rumors had spread that he'd been disloyal to his land, his kingdom, and his people, and everyone in Jinu turned against him, even his own siblings. Huiqing was forced to confess to the public because if he didn't, Qianfan threatened to burn his siblings alive.

Jinhai turned the pages, reading each and every word, and eventually reached the page where Qiang wrote about her voyage—the voyage that changed her life.

I have reached the kingdom where Xiuying resides. I had informed her beforehand of my visit, and to my surprise, Xiuying came with royal favors to meet me at the harbor, despite how terrible I've treated her in the past. She is married to Prince Zhang Wei of the Baoshu Kingdom, and he loves her like I've never seen my own son love his wife. She reminds me of her mother, but Xiuying is much more human than her. For Heaven's sake, she refused to even let me apologize! Instead, she welcomed me with open arms and gave me a place to stay at her castle.

Xiaofan is also living with her. Xiuying searched everywhere for her after discovering that her parents had also abandoned her, eventually finding her at a run-down orphanage and bringing her here. I knew all this, and I should've done something—anything—other than promote it and encourage my son, but I didn't. All I did was sit back and did nothing. I'm no less of a monster than my own son.

But I'm glad they're doing better... even after their parents took everything from them. They seem happy, successful, a queen and a princess... no thanks to me. To this day, I regret what I've done. Both of them suffered greatly to get to where they are today.

Xiuying's final days in Jinu are still nothing but emotional baggage. She'd still hear the angry roars of my son and the hateful cries of her own mother. Such a tragic experience for a young child. She'd freeze and lose control of her body whenever memories of the past crept in, and despite being surrounded by loved ones now, part of her would always feel like she isn't good enough, that she'd be abandoned again one day.

Xiaofan's memories aren't much better, even more unsettling, I'd say. If her memories of the raggedy orphanage and the evil headmistress weren't enough to send her for the hills, then the assault that she'd experi-

enced on the streets by a bunch of thugs certainly was. And though she eventually managed to escape it all, she'd still wake up frightened by her nightmares of the past. But she tries to remain strong! Oh, she always tries to remain strong. But when she doesn't and begins to cry... my heart goes out to her.

I have failed to protect my granddaughters.

I have failed as a human being.

Don't get me wrong, Jinhai. Your sisters did come to the castle when they found out about you and your sister, Xiaosheng. I guess they were scared of what your father would do to you both if they didn't save you. And I don't blame them. But your father kicked them both out and threatened them with death if they were to try and come back.

Zhang and Han were both ready to attack, but your sisters stopped them. They believe in you, Jinhai. They believe that you have the power to overturn your father without any bloodshed. Prove them right.

Over the years, your father has only thought about himself, his power, and his status. He has murdered people for the sake of murdering them and nothing else—brothers, fathers, sons. And your mother is aware of all this, aware of all the evil doings, but she chooses to stay silent and support her husband, like an honorable wife should. But this is wrong. This is all wrong.

The hunger that Qianfan has for blood and tears is going to destroy this kingdom one day unless you stop him. And by the looks of it, the kingdom is already falling apart.

When I arrived back at the kingdom, I wanted to tell

you about your sisters, Jinhai. I wanted to tell you that they're still alive and want to see you defeat your father. But when my son found out what I was up to, he smashed a glass vase and threatened to cut me with the sharpest piece. He has never spoken to me in that tone before. I must've done something wrong as a mother.

But I'm not scared. I know he will fall on his face one day. And when he does, I'll be laughing. From where? I do not know, for Qianfan has put a death card on my life, and I don't know when I'll ever see the light of day again.

Hopefully, you'll find this journal before he does and make sure that everyone knows the truth. If you don't, my son will set it on fire alongside my body.

If my instincts are right, and if this is goodbye, always remember that your grandmother loves you and Xiaosheng. And if you ever get a chance to meet your sisters, tell them that I am truly sorry and that I've tried to make things right. But sometimes, it's not possible when it comes to Qianfan. Tell Xiaosheng about your sisters. How Xiuying loves to paint, just like she does. And how Xiaofan's best friend, Fia, is planning on joining the Jinu Kingdom very soon. Those two were inseparable at the orphanage.

Lastly, Jinhai, don't forget to believe in yourself. You have the ability to feel what others feel, and that is a rare gift. Connect with your people, and let them guide you to victory.

Jinhai turned the page to find it blank. The pages were all covered with his tears, and his eyes were swollen. He was in a state of shock. Could his father have really murdered his grandmother? His own mother?

Qiang died three days after she came back from the voyage, and she was perfectly healthy when she did. She definitely didn't die from health complications like his father had told everyone she did. There was also zero sadness on the king's face, completely apathetic, like he didn't even care about the death of his own mother!

Jinhai felt dizzy. Nauseous and sick from what he'd just found out. He got up and sat down on his grandmother's bed, placing his head in his hands. He closed his eyes and took a deep breath. The first face that popped in front of his eyes was Fia's, and he smiled over the fact that the reason why he'd felt so connected to Fia was because the Universe sent her into his sister's life before he even knew about her. It *wasn't* just a coincidence that he found himself attracted to her.

"Fia! Dinner!" He glanced over at the clock. "I'm late!"

Jinhai had been so focused on finding out the truth that he'd completely forgotten! He quickly placed the journal back in between the floorboards, carefully sealing it so no one else would suspect that something was underneath.

When he stood back up, his eyes caught sight of a small teacup that sat on Qiang's desk. There was a green liquid inside, almost clear. Green tea, maybe?

And a delicate flower sat at the bottom center. On closer inspection, Jinhai's stomach dropped.

That was no ordinary flower. Nerium oleander. A poisonous flower!

And beside the cup was a note.

Making temporary amends, Mother. Night, night.

Qianfan

CHAPTER
SEVEN

ANOTHER TWO HOURS HAD GONE BY, AND IT WAS ALMOST midnight. Jiayi and Fia wanted to continue waiting for Jinhai, but Xiaosheng insisted that they start without him. She was starving, after all, and Fia's stomach was also growling.

"He probably fell asleep or something. Everything's getting cold, and if I don't eat something soon, I will pass out!" Xiaosheng exclaimed.

"Can you be a little more dramatic?" Jiayi asked.

Suddenly, they heard footsteps approaching the front door of the dining room.

"That must be Jinhai!" Xiaosheng screamed in excitement, more so for her stomach than for her brother's appearance. "What took you so long?"

But the face that walked in didn't belong to Jinhai. It belonged to someone she'd never expect to see again, to someone she didn't want to see again.

"Nothing, I simply was not invited, my dear daughter," the queen answered in a taunting tone.

"I am *not* your daughter, and you are *not* my mother. No, you were not invited, and you are certainly not welcome here!" Xiaosheng shouted at Daiyu, crossing her arms over her chest.

"Have you forgotten your manners, Jiayi? No offering for the queen's arrival?" Daiyu turned to face Jiayi and asked.

Jiayi stood up with her heart beating fast against her chest, but before she could say anything, Daiyu started to walk toward Fia.

"You know, word travels fast in this castle. I don't know why, but you all seem to forget that this is *my* castle, *my* kingdom, and I know *everything* that happens within these walls," Daiyu firmly claimed while looking from Fia to Jiayi and back. "And you think you have gotten yourself a prince? Ha! What a joke! My son is *never* going to marry some low-class trash like you." Daiyu glared into Fia's eyes and smirked.

"That's where you're wrong, Mother," Jinhai jumped in when he entered the room.

His sleeves were rolled up, his eyes were a little red

and swollen, but his voice remained firm, strong. But his appearance at that moment startled everyone in the room.

"You may be the queen of this kingdom, Mother, but that is all you are," Jinhai spoke and walked toward Fia. "You don't know the prince, and you certainly don't know your own son. The woman standing before you is going to take your place very soon. So, I suggest that you show some respect if you don't want your future to be in jeopardy."

Daiyu was surprised. Jinhai had *never* spoken to her like that before, never disrespected her like that before. "How *dare* you speak to your own mother so dishonorably?" Daiyu shouted.

"Mother? Are you serious? You have abandoned us. You can't just walk back in whenever it's convenient for you and expect us to respect you. You mean nothing to us anymore. You and your demented husband can both die, for all I care." Then he pointed toward the door. "Now, please leave, and never come back."

Xiaosheng drew an evil grin on her face. She loved seeing her awful mother get what she deserved. Daiyu stood there speechless for a minute, and then stormed out of the room, along with the guards and maids who had accompanied her.

The room fell silent after she left. Jinhai wrapped his arms around Fia and assured her that she had nothing to worry about. "I'm sorry I was late."

Turning to Jiayi, he asked her to bring in some tea as he had important matters to discuss with them all.

"What is it, Jinhai? You're making me anxious!" Xiaosheng was the first to say. "Is everything okay?"

"It is now," Jinhai answered mysteriously, still holding Fia's hand.

"If this is important, maybe I should leave you three alone. Besides, it's already pretty late," Fia whispered quietly, still shaken by what the queen had said to her.

"No, you need to hear this, too. I want you to be here, Fia. Please."

"You seem so tired," Fia pointed out.

"I am, but it's okay," Jinhai replied while looking down.

Jiayi came in with some hot oolong tea for everyone and sat down beside Xiaosheng.

"Now, can you please elaborate on what has been happening? Jinhai, you have made me so worried!" Jiayi urged.

Jinhai took a deep breath, then after taking a sip of his tea, he started to unfold the events that had occurred earlier today. He explained every detail, from his meeting with Huiqing to discovering Qiang's journal, and finally, to exposing the truth behind the death of his grandmother.

"I know this is a lot to understand, to accept, but look on the bright side, we know the truth. And we can bring justice to others and fight for what's right.

Xiaosheng, you've always complained about wanting an older sister. Well, now you have two, two who love you dearly from afar. We must take the kingdom away from my conniving father. We shall *not* let our grandmother's sacrifice go to waste!"

Xiaosheng wiped her tears and agreed, muttering, "Yes."

"Xiaofan was my best friend at the orphanage, and we used to share everything. When she first came in, she was very quiet and had a hard time adjusting to how things functioned there. She was very strong and brave, but something in her broke after she was attacked, and after she left, something similar happened to me. Two men came into the courtyard when I was alone and grabbed me. I tried to fight them off, but I wasn't strong enough. They were huge! But luckily, Xiaofan sent over an army of guards that came to my rescue, and shortly after that, the orphanage dismantled, and all the girls were sent to different kingdoms. That's how I came here. Xiaofan specifically told me that Jinu would be the safest place for me. I didn't know why at the time, but now it's pretty obvious... because of you two." She nodded her head toward Jinhai and Xiaosheng.

"The more I think about it, the more I am unable to understand the mysterious ways that the Universe works, but the one thing I can say for sure is that those who go out of their way to help others always get rewarded in the end," Jiayi said with a grin, and then added. "The Universe will always have your back, Fia. I just know it."

After Fia headed back home, Jiayi and Xiaosheng proceeded to their own rooms to get some rest, promising each other that they wouldn't tell a soul about what they had just learned from Jinhai.

Jinhai stood alone in his room with a solemn heart. He always knew that one day, he had to become a king, but now, that reality was absolutely necessary. He just had to figure out how to do it. He knew his father was much more powerful than him, but Qianfan was also a fool. Jinhai would outsmart him somehow. Maybe Lixin and Haitao would have some words of encouragement. He'd go and talk to them in the morning. For now, he wanted to let himself bask in the sorrow of losing those who've loved him. If anything, the overthrow of Qianfan would be the way to avenge them.

THE NEXT MORNING, JINHAI woke up early to the bright rays of sunlight burning his face. He opened his eyes and realized how different things were going to be from now on, how today was going to be the first chapter in his new life. For once, he was not oblivious to his family's wretched past. He strictly forbade everyone around him to talk about the news that he had unveiled. While many of the castle residents despised the king and queen, many were still loyal to them.

Jinhai jumped out of bed and quickly got dressed. He then left to go see Lixin and Haitao. It was still early in the morning when he arrived at their home, and he walked in on them eating breakfast.

"Jinhai, what a surprise, my son! Come, grab yourself a plate!" Lixin welcomed him in.

"Why the long face?" Haitao asked.

"Is everything okay?" Lixin followed up, and within a matter of minutes, Jinhai told them everything.

"Lixin, you never knew anything about my sisters?" Jinhai asked.

Lixin sighed, and then replied, "I had heard some rumors around town, but I was never certain, so I figured it was best to not even mention them to you. It would only hurt that much more if they were false."

"We're always here for you. You know that, right? Let us know whatever you need, whenever you need, and we got you. You don't have to go through this alone," Haitao firmly said and gave Jinhai a pat on the back.

"I know. That's why I'm here. I won't be able to do this alone. And Haitao, no need to stop cracking jokes. Sometimes a little bit of distraction is good during rough times."

"Always." Haitao beamed.

"With time, everything is going to unfold in a way that works out in your favor, Jinhai. But for now, you need to take it one day at a time. You're stressed. I can tell. And that usually causes you to make hasty decisions. Once you take the time to clear your mind, I'm sure the solution will be much clearer to you," Lixin explained.

"And how do I do that?" Jinhai muttered.

"Well, if you ask me," Haitao jumped in, "I've seen the way you handle stress, and it is *not* good, my friend. Father is right. You need to relax a bit. Why not spend some time with the girl next door? You know, her name starts with an F and rhymes with Pia." He started jabbing Jinhai on the side while chuckling, and Jinhai flailed his own arms at him.

Jinhai had never been much of a romanticist, so when it came to spending time with someone of the opposite gender or surprising her with some big romantic gesture, he was utterly confused. But he wanted to do *something*. He didn't want to become like his father, whose greatest gesture was having a child with the woman he loved and then throwing it away. No, he needed to be better than that!

Then he remembered something. The small wooden terrace near the lake that he and Xiaosheng had built when they were kids so they could sit and watch the birds. And even better? The terrace was far away from the castle, kept hidden from even the guards and maids! This was where he used to go with his sister to escape the problems of the castle, a place where they could just sit for hours and hours without a worry in the world.

And it had been years since he'd visited, and since

the place held such sentiment in his heart, he decided that it would be the perfect place to take Fia. After all, there was nothing more romantic than showing her a little part of his world that mattered a lot to him.

CHAPTER
EIGHT

IT WAS HALF PAST NOON ON A SUNNY WINTER DAY WHEN Jinhai arrived at Fia's home. The sun was shining through fluffy clouds in the blue sky, and birds were chirping songs of praise overhead. Jinhai knocked on the door, crossing his fingers in hopes that Fia would answer. He'd never been more nervous in his life.

"Oh, hi!" Fia greeted, surprised to see Jinhai.

"H—what's on your face?" Jinhai stopped talking. *What's wrong with you? You don't say that to a woman! Idiot!* "S-sorry, I didn't mean it like that."

But Fia just giggled. "You must be talking about

the chocolate smeared all over my face." Jinhai nodded. "Let's just say, chocolate-covered dumplings sounded like a good idea, but it's definitely pretty disgusting." She giggled again. "So, what brings you here?"

"Nothing much," Jinhai smirked. "I just came by to see if you were busy. I thought I'd show you a place that means a lot to me. A special place."

"Nope, not busy at all! I just, you know, need to clean up a bit before I go out in public." Then she thought about what Jinhai had just said. "What special place?"

"It's a surprise." Jinhai winked. "I guess you'll just have to come with me to find out."

"You're such a tease. Let me go get changed, and I'll meet you outside."

Jinhai nodded and walked back to his carriage to wait for her. A few minutes later, Fia walked out looking like a completely different person! Her face was as clean as clean can be, her hair was tied up in intricate braids, and she carried a small woven basket on her petite wrist. Jinhai could feel his heart beating faster and faster as she approached him.

"You clean up good," he complimented.

"Anything for you, my prince." And Fia bowed.

After a long and bumpy ride on an old dirt road, they finally reached the lake. They stepped out, and Fia's eyes widened with amazement. She was surrounded by beautiful cherry blossom trees that wrapped around the lake, white doves that circled above her head, and the grass was much greener and softer than what she'd been used to. And over to her left, there was an old oak tree that had a wooden platform built into it with stairs leading upwards.

"This is incredible," she whispered as she continued to look around, basking in the petals that fell over her as she did.

"It really is. Xiaosheng and I used to come here all the time to get away from our parents. Besides you, no one else knows about it."

"I'm very flattered." Fia bowed again.

Jinhai grabbed Fia by the hand and led her up the staircase. As they climbed, she smiled at the incredible view of the lake and the different colors of the sunset. The sky had turned into shades of pink, yellow, and orange, and Fia felt like she was living inside a fairytale.

"A year ago, I would've never imagined my life turning out the way that it did. I was just a young man trying to get through life and make sure my father doesn't ruin my life. Now I'm preparing to take down my father and find my long-lost sisters. It's crazy how much things can change with time. Sometimes for the better, sometimes for the worse."

"Well?" Fia asked.

"Well, what?"

"Has your life changed for the better or for the worse?"

"Hard to say, really." Then Jinhai wrapped his arm around her waist and pulled her in close. "But with you by my side, I'd have to say for the better, much better." He slowly leaned his face down toward hers and planted a kiss on her lips. He had never kissed anyone before, and he didn't know what he was doing, but Fia's lips just felt so... so familiar that he didn't want to pull away.

"I could say the same about my life. It's not every day that a poor orphan girl gets to be with a royal prince," Fia whispered when they slightly parted.

"I hope I'm able to make life better for you." Fia nodded, and Jinhai leaned in to kiss her once more. When they finally parted again, Jinhai continued. "I want to apologize for yesterday, for being late. I know there's no excuse on my part, inviting you over and then disappearing for hours. If it wasn't for me, Daiyu may have never made an appearance. I'm sorry I wasn't there to protect you from her. I should've been there." He pulled her in for a hug. "Just know that no matter what she says or what anyone says, my heart belongs to you, and I'd choose you over a princess any day."

"Jinhai, it's okay. You have nothing to apologize for. You stuck up for me, and that's what matters."

Jinhai let out a sigh of relief and muttered, "Thank you for understanding."

"Always."

Jinhai then climbed down and started a fire to make some tea.

"You know how to do this?" Fia asked in shock.

"Yes, plus a lot of other things. When it comes to

making tea, I am considered an expert." Jinhai laughed.

"Well, then I have the perfect thing to go with it!" Fia made her way down also and laid down a red sheet for them on top of the grass. "Good thing I brought some dumplings with me."

"I was wondering what you had inside that basket. Thought it might've been a human head or something," Jinhai joked.

The sun soon started to set, and the lighting dimmed as time passed.

"Sometimes I wish I could just get a break from all the constants problems in my life," Jinhai pondered while pouring the tea into tiny cups. "As I grow older and older, I realize how much different life is from when I was just a child. The scary tales that I used to read in books are now all coming to life."

"I get how you feel, but letting uncontrollable situations run our lives is definitely not the right way to go. Instead, it's better to use those dark moments as fuel to make a change."

"I guess you're right. You always know the right things to say, Fia." Jinhai took a sip of his tea and sighed. "I really needed this."

"Me, too." Fia smiled. "And this tea is magnificent. You really are an expert!"

"Told you so." Jinhai laughed.

An hour later, the sun had completely set, and it was time to head home. On the way back, Jinhai saw the fireflies around them glimmer against the night sky, like tiny stars were floating around them. And in that moment, he knew that they belonged together. That the Universe had put Fia in his life for a reason.

When they arrived at Fia's home, she turned to him and said, "You know, whenever I think about Xiaofan, it makes me think about how ironic it is that every moment in our lives is connected somehow to what's ahead of us. How every person who crosses our lives brings some sort of significance. It's crazy if you really stop to think about it."

"Yeah, but I'm not complaining." He gave her one last kiss on the cheek and hopped back inside the carriage to head back to the castle. He was slowly falling in love with her, and in the past, this would've been his sign to run in the opposite direction. But he had a good feeling about Fia, and he couldn't even begin to imagine his life without her.

When he finally arrived back, he walked straight toward his room. He didn't want to risk the possibility of running into his parents or any of their loyal minions. He just wanted to find Jiayi and Xiaosheng. Hopefully, they're still awake. But when he went into their rooms, he found them both empty. Heart pounding, he started to get worried.

What if Qianfan got to them already? What if he knows that I know? They could be dead by now!

Then he heard footsteps behind him, and when he spun around, expecting to see his father's cynical smile, he saw his sister instead.

"Where were you? I was looking for you! And

Jiayi!" Jinhai exclaimed as soon as he saw her. "I thought our father had gotten to you or something and sent you away."

"Oh, stop being paranoid. I just went for a walk out in the garden with Jiayi," Xiaosheng told him. "Besides, I can take care of myself."

"Why do you have a weird smile on your face? What are you up to?"

"I have to tell you something."

"Okay... What is it?"

"No, wait. No! It's not something I can tell you," Xiaosheng corrected herself.

"What? What's wrong with you?"

"It's something I have to show you!"

"Okay...?"

Xiaosheng then closed her eyes, and it even confused Jinhai even more.

"Are you okay?" he asked but was ignored. Then after about two seconds, the book that was sitting on the table beside them started to levitate over his head. "What? Xiaosheng, what's this?"

"I got my power! I got my power!" She jumped up and down with excitement, her focus dwindling from the book, and eventually, it fell onto Jinhai's head.

It stung, but he didn't care. His baby sister finally got her power, and he couldn't be prouder.

Suddenly, he heard a bang, a thud, followed by a faint scream.

"What was that?" Jinhai asked.

But Xiaosheng just shrugged. "I didn't hear

anything."

"Hm, must've been an animal or something. Anyway, Xiaosheng, that's fantastic! I'm so happy for you!" Jinhai gave his sister a bear hug. "You are finally growing up, but it still seems like you were born just yesterday," he whispered.

"Oh, don't get all emotional on me now!" Xiaosheng teased. "Just expect things to be thrown at you whenever you annoy me."

"You do that, and I'll drown you in a sea of water," Jinhai teased back.

"Really?"

"Maybe." Then he winked.

Xiaosheng getting her power could not have come at a better time. Jinhai needed all the strength and support that he could get during this time, but it also made him realize how much of an emotional toll his sister must've gone through with everything happening around them. A part of him felt guilty for putting his sister through so much. He was supposed to protect her, not expose her to the tragedies of reality. But at the same time, she was now officially a member of the magical Jinu Kingdom, and he promised himself that he would teach her, and himself, how to use her power well.

THE NEXT MORNING, JINHAI DIDN'T WASTE ANY TIME. HE felt like he was in the right space mentally, and he knew it was time to come back to reality and plot out his revenge against his father's reign of terror.

But first, a visit to see Huiqing. It had been a few days since he'd requested the guards to send him a few more supplies, and he wanted to make sure the man was still alive. He walked to the front door of the prison and found the same guards standing there.

"All the changes done?" Jinhai asked discretely.

"Yes, sir," they both answered simultaneously and unlocked the iron gate for Jinhai to enter.

And as soon as he walked in, he noticed all the visible changes. Warm blankets were distributed to all the prisoners, the leaking pipes were sealed, and the odor that previously lingered in the air now smelled like fresh mint.

Jinhai walked toward Huiqing's cell and sat down in front of him.

"Something in you has changed, my child," Huiqing whispered.

"A lot has changed, actually," Jinhai replied and told him all about Qiang's journal and what she had written inside.

"I am happy for your sisters. They deserved every bit of it." Huiqing smiled weakly.

"And you were right," Jinhai continued. "Grandmother's death was not just a coincidence or a health complication. She was poisoned, and I have proof. My father was a fool to not clean up after his own mess. And now, he is going to pay for trying to play God."

"The best punishment for someone like Qianfan

would be to take away his power, the one thing that makes him invincible," Huiqing told him.

"It is time we dethrone him. The people of Jinu are already against him, and once the truth comes out, they will join me and stand up against him. I will reveal the truth about their precious king, and I will clear your name, Huiqing. I will make sure that you get out of here alive, one way or another."

"I hope you do. You are a man of your word, but remember to always have a backup plan. You don't know Qianfan and how evil he can truly be. Perhaps you can join forces with your sisters. You are not the only one whom Qianfan has wronged. Together, you can all unite and take down your father."

Jinhai nodded and bowed, thanking Huiqing for all that he had done. "Stay strong, Huiqing. This will all be over soon." He stood up and headed toward the exit, hearing shouts of praise from the others as he passed them.

When he got back to his room, he immediately started drawing up his plans. He knew the people trusted him, and he definitely had the support of Haitao and Lixin, but Huiqing was right. He needed the powers of his magical sisters. It's the only thing that's powerful enough against Qianfan. Plus, his sisters deserved to know what's happening in their own kingdom, so he pulled out a quill and started to write.

Dearest Sisters,

My entire life, I have believed that I was the eldest...

until recently. Our father is a cunning man, how he was able to cover up his wrongdoings all these years, the torture that he had inflicted on the both of you. I feel utterly ashamed for not having discovered this earlier, for not being there for the both of you. But now I know the truth, thanks to Mei's sister and Huiqing. I'm sure you both know them well.

I think it's time we all take a stand against Father. End this misery for our family and the people struggling on the streets of the kingdom. It is time his reign ends. It is time that the people of Jinu live under a ruler who has their best interest at heart.

I must dethrone the king, but to do that, I will need your help. Xiaosheng will need your help. There is a reason that I found out about you and a reason we all have powers… because it's in the Universe's plan to reunite us and make a difference in this world. I know you're probably both very happy where you are, and I want nothing less than for your lives to stay that way, but I'm sure, that like me, you are both also hungry for revenge. Plus, your little sister will be thrilled to finally meet you.

Xiaofan, I have met Fia, your best friend. And it just so happens that I have fallen in love with her. Life is too short to live in fear under our father.

I hope you both consider joining me in this fight.

Your brother,

Jinhai

He then sealed the letter with wax, rolled it into a scroll, and walked down to the harbor to deliver it himself. He refused to take any chances when it came to this. It was too important to put into the trust of someone else.

"I have a plan," Jinhai announced when he walked into Lixin's shop afterwards and told him all the details.

"Are you sure the military will support you in this? What if they retaliate? The chief *is* your father's ally, after all. He is *never* going to betray him," Lixin questioned with concern.

"I've done my research, and besides the chief, every other soldier is on my side. They all despise my father, and they've all been waiting for the day when they can finally be free from his grasp," Jinhai explained.

"Sounds promising."

"I also wrote to my sisters. I need their powers in this fight. I am hopeful that they show up," Jinhai said.

"So, what do we do now?" Lixin asked.

"We wait for a response, and then we take action."

Lixin had doubts that he didn't voice. He knew that Jinhai was doing the right thing. This was what the kingdom needed, what the people needed, but Qianfan was *not* someone who would easily back down in defeat. Jinhai's approach to wait might give Qianfan a slight advantage and attack, but Jinhai needed support, and that was what Lixin needed to give him. This was the ultimate test of his patience, and he tried not to let his worries get the best of him.

"Jinhai, I have known you ever since you were just a little boy. You are much stronger than you give yourself credit for, and the only way your plan will succeed is if you believe in it. Don't doubt yourself," Lixin said when he noticed Jinhai rubbing his hands together. He usually did that whenever his thoughts conflicted with each other.

"Thank you, Lixin. I will do my best."

THREE DAYS HAD GONE BY, AND JINHAI STILL HADN'T HEARD from his sisters. He was on the verge of losing hope, when suddenly, he heard a knock on the door.

"Letter for you, Prince Jinhai," a guard spoke from outside the door.

Jinhai rushed over to open it, quickly yanked the scroll out of the guard's hands, and slammed the door shut. He then ripped it open as fast as he could and read.

Beloved Jinhai,

We hope this letter reaches you before we do, and we are both so proud of you for taking a stand against our awful father. And to be honest, nothing would make us happier than to watch him burn. You have our full support, and however this fight ends, at least we are all together.

We hope to arrive at Jinu soon, and we can't wait to finally meet you and Xiaosheng.

Your sisters,

Xiuying and Xiaofan

NINE

Hope, a simple four-lettered word that makes people trust in the unknown and hope for the best against any evil.

That is exactly what Jinhai had done. He had hoped for his sisters to show up for him, and now he was hoping that everything would go as planned, that justice would be served without any bloodshed.

He kept the scroll hidden inside his room and decided to keep the news of his sisters' arrival to himself. He wanted to meet with them alone first without generating a crowd, and he wanted to give Xiaosheng the same experience.

He didn't know what he was going to do when he faces his father. He had originally envisioned himself speaking to his father in a calm and civil manner, but that idea was quickly brushed out the door when he realized that the king would never be reasonable. With Qianfan, there was never a dull moment; tantrums and threats of death always did the talking for him. But still, Jinhai was nervous. His father always managed to demean him as a child. What would make it any different now?

While Jinhai was occupied with his thoughts, Xiaosheng and Fia were getting ready for brunch over at Fia's home. Xiaosheng was super excited to spend some time alone with her. Whenever Jinhai was around, he took all of Fia's attention, but now, Xiaosheng had her all for herself, and she liked feeling like she had a sister. She wondered what it would feel like if her blood sisters ever came to visit. Would it be like meeting a stranger? Or would she feel right at home with them?

On her way out the door, she turned back around to say goodbye to Jiayi. She hadn't seen her since last night, which was odd since Jiayi was *always* around. But Xiaosheng was in a hurry and didn't give it another thought. Besides, Jiayi had a lot of responsibilities in the kingdom. She was probably just busy.

Xiaosheng checked Jiayi's room one last time, and when she didn't see her, she left to go meet Fia. After riding through the busy streets and rocky pathways, Xiaosheng finally reached her destination and was greeted with open arms.

Fia's home was small, more of a cottage than a house, with wooden floors, mustard-colored walls, herbs planted in every corner, and the windows were all open to let in the cool breeze. It reminded her of one of her doll homes that Xiaosheng had growing up, and she remembered how she often wished that she was tiny enough to walk through one of them. She giggled as the thought crossed her mind.

"What's so funny?" Fia asked, placing a basket of baked buns in front of Xiaosheng along with a pot of warm tea.

"Oh, it's nothing. Your house just reminds me of one of the dollhouses I had when I was younger. It feels like I'm inside one of them."

Fia chuckled. "I never thought about it that way before. It does look like one."

"So, how did you know that Jinhai was the one for you?" Xiaosheng asked. "How do you know when you've found that special person?"

Fia looked outside the window, noticing the birds flying in pairs across the bright blue sky. "I don't know how to put it in words, exactly, but you just feel it in your heart when you meet someone who's right for you. You feel like you can talk to them about anything, and you feel like the best version of yourself around them. Does that make sense?"

"I guess. I hope I can find my own true love one day." Xiaosheng sighed.

"Don't feel like you have to rush into it. You will meet countless people in your lifetime, some good, some bad. Some deserving of your love, others not so much. Most are going to take you for granted and then just leave. But the ones who stick by your side during all the low points in your life are the ones worth keeping." Fia held Xiaosheng's hand tightly. "Don't sacrifice your own life for someone else. Just keep that in mind."

"You're right, Fia. Sometimes I just get so caught up in growing up and wanting what others around me have that I forget I still have many years to live. Thank you. You've been like a big sister to me."

The ride back to the castle made Xiaosheng feel anxious. Her heart was racing, and she didn't really know why. But whenever it did, something bad usually happened right after. Hopefully, her intuition was wrong this time. When she walked in through the front door, she looked for Jiayi. Most nights, she'd just be in the kitchen, cooking up something delicious, but when she found the kitchen empty, she felt a wave of sadness.

"Have you seen Jiayi?" Xiaosheng asked one of the maids instead.

"I haven't seen her all day," the maid replied.

"What do you mean?" Xiaosheng asked.

"I mean, I don't know. Look for her somewhere else," the maid hissed angrily and walked away.

Xiaosheng didn't respond, but she overheard the maid whisper something to another as she left. She continued to look for Jiayi throughout the castle, but Jiayi was nowhere to be found. This was very unlike her, disappearing without saying a word, and Xiaosheng immediately started jumping to the worst possible conclusions.

When she arrived back at Jiayi's room, she noticed that the door was already open. And when she walked in, the room was a mess! It so was unlike Jiayi, who was usually the most organized person she'd ever met. It looked like a fight or a fit of rage had taken place here, like someone had purposefully smashed everything inside. All of her things were thrown from one side to the other, the sheets were torn and scattered all over the floor, and the vases that used to carry the most beautiful of flowers were all smashed against the ground, glass shards sprinkled throughout the room.

Something bad had happened here. Something really bad. Xiaosheng quickly rushed to Jinhai's room and started banging violently against the door.

"Open up, Jinhai!" Xiaosheng's voice was in such a panic.

Jinhai rushed toward the door to open it, and Xiaosheng quickly rushed in and slammed the door behind her shut as she paced around the room from one end to the other.

"Jiayi is gone! Jiayi is gone!" Xiaosheng repeated frantically.

"Xiaosheng, I don't understand. Can you calm

down for a second?" Jinhai asked, but Xiaosheng continued pacing back and forth. Jinhai then held her by the shoulders and forced her to stand still. "What's going on?"

"I haven't seen Jiayi since yesterday, and I tried to look for her this morning, but I couldn't find her anywhere. When I came back from Fia's, I tried looking for her in the kitchen, but she still wasn't there. And the other maids were whispering, whispering something that they clearly didn't want me to know about. Then I went into her room..." Xiaosheng stuttered and broke into tears.

"You went into her room and then?" Jinhai urged his sister to continue.

"She wasn't in there either, and her room was an absolute mess! You know Jiayi would *never* leave it like that. Something happened in there, a fight, a struggle. I think someone took Jiayi!"

There was no doubt in Jinhai's mind that this was the work of his parents. Someone must've overheard them talking and took Jiayi as collateral. A bird couldn't even move around the castle without them finding out.

"I will find her, Xiaosheng," Jinhai told his baby sister as he wiped down her tears and hugged her tight. "She's going to be here with you soon, I promise. But I need you to stay right here until I come back. Do *not* go anywhere else! Lock the door and the windows, and I will be back as soon as I can."

Jinhai pulled away and headed toward the door

when he heard a knock. He opened it and found a maid standing there with her head down.

"Jiayi was taken by the queen," she whispered. "She is going to be executed tomorrow. Please don't tell anyone that you heard this from me." Luckily, Xiaosheng didn't hear anything, and Jinhai intended to keep it that way.

Executed? Jinhai thought to himself as he closed the door behind him and marched toward his parents' room.

AFTER JINHAI EMBARRASSED DAIYU WITHOUT ANY HESITATION that night, she had fallen into a pit of self-doubt that she thought she would never experience again in her life. That incident took her back to the night when Xiuying tried to take her own life. It reminded her of how Mei had spoken to her and how much she'd despised that, and now, years later, her own son—her own blood—was doing the exact same thing, like he had absolutely no respect for her. She blamed Jiayi and the way she'd raised him. To Daiyu, Jiayi and Mei were cut from the same cloth.

Daiyu felt like her children loved Jiayi more than her, and it made her feel insignificant. How dare Jinhai talk back to her like that? She was his mother! Someone had to pay for his disrespect, and Jiayi—their pathetic nanny—was the perfect *prey*.

"You know what I hate most about my life?" Daiyu

asked cynically when Jiayi walked back into her room the night that Xiaosheng discovered her power to discover the queen sitting on her bed. "It's women who try to take my children away from me. First, it was Mei, the maid who tried to make Xiuying her own, and now, it's you, the *bitch* trying to take Xiaosheng and Jinhai. It's always *someone*, isn't it?" Daiyu hissed with a sinister laugh. "But women like you forget that you can *never* be a mother to them; you can *never* take my place!" Daiyu shouted and smashed a vase against the floor, glass shards flying off in all directions. "Women who turn children against their mothers deserve to rot, and that is *exactly* what will happen to you."

"I never turned them against you. I have only given them the love and affection that you failed to!" Jiayi pleaded.

"Liar! I will personally make sure that you will *never* see the light of day again! Guards, take her to the dungeon!" Daiyu ordered and left the room with her maids.

"No!" Jiayi shouted, stepping back as the guards approached her. Her feet were bloody as the shards cut through her skin. "Please, don't!" She screamed for mercy and tried to fight off the guards, but they held onto her arms tightly and dragged her to the basement.

Jiayi was kept inside the dark cell in front of Huiqing. Huiqing could hear her cries and tried to comfort her, but nothing helped. Jiayi was different than Mei. She was easily frightened, sensitive, and this was taking a toll on her. She hoped that Xiaosheng and Jinhai would soon find her, but that hope was dwindling as the days passed. This was her fate now. She always hated working for the queen.

"WHERE COULD SHE BE?" JINHAI ASKED HIMSELF AS HE stormed toward the king and queen's quarters of the castle. When he reached there, to his surprise, they were both sitting together and dining on the grand terrace, which only made Jinhai fume even more. But when Daiyu saw him, she simply smiled.

"My son, to what do I owe the pleasure of this visit?" Daiyu asked, her sickly tone exuding fakeness.

"Why did you take Jiayi? And to execute her? What's the matter with you?" Jinhai screamed in resentment toward the woman who birthed him.

"I can do anything as the Queen of Jinu, stupid child!" Daiyu cackled while clapping her hands.

"Forget Jiayi, my son! We are celebrating this kingdom's first execution. Come, join us. This event will go down in history!" Qianfan chimed in jovially.

"How many more lives need to perish for your own amusement? This is injustice!" Jinhai exclaimed.

"There *is* no injustice, you fool! Jiayi is nothing more than a filthy servant who wants our gold and our throne by *brainwashing* our children. Trust me, Jinhai, she doesn't love you or your annoying sister. She is only doing this for herself," Daiyu declared.

"No! She has been more of a mother to us than you have ever been, than you ever will be! And you're right. Tomorrow *will* go down in history, but not for the reason you think. I will do *everything* in my power to prevent that from happening!" Jinhai hissed as he violently pushed away the cup of tea that was being offered to him, causing the glass to smash against the floor.

"You are all words and no action, my son. You are as soft as a feather. A wimp. A coward. Ever since you were just a baby. You are no match for me." Qianfan sneered while Daiyu stared at Jinhai with hatred in her eyes as he stormed out of the room.

"Where could she be? Where could she be?" he kept whispering to himself. Then he paused. "The prison! Of course!"

He rushed down to the basement, and when he reached the entrance, he found six military guards standing there with sharp swords in their hands, guarding the iron gate.

"Let me in," Jinhai ordered.

"No one is allowed to enter this part of the castle. We have strict orders from the king," one of the guards answered.

"I am the prince of this kingdom. I command you to open this gate at once!"

"I'm afraid we cannot do that. If we let you inside, the king will have our heads," another guard muttered.

"Ugh! I hate my father and his tyrannical ways!" Jinhai screamed at the top of his lungs and stormed back toward his room.

It was almost dawn when he passed by Jiayi's room and saw tiny droplets of blood on the carpet. His parents had gone too far this time, and he swore to himself that he will make them pay for all of it, no matter what it took.

His mind muddy and his blood still boiling, he went to his own room and found it closed but unlocked. Jinhai quickly rushed to check on the scroll. Luckily, it was still where he'd left it, untouched, untampered with. Feeling a rush of relief, he then sat by the window and watched the color change in the sky before dozing off.

A FEW HOURS LATER, HE WOKE UP TO XIAOSHENG'S VOICE AS she walked into the room with breakfast and closed the door.

"What time is it?" Jinhai asked, startled.

"Almost noon," Xiaosheng answered before she hesitantly asked, "Find anything?"

Jinhai nodded and spoke before he could stop himself. "Jiayi is still alive, but she has been imprisoned by Daiyu. She's fine for now, but they plan to execute her, and I must stop it before it's too late."

"She can't do that! If she does, I will *never* forgive her. Never!" Xiaosheng began dripping tears from her eyes.

"And...," Jinhai started, quickly changing the subject, but paused.

"And?" Xiaosheng repeated while she sniffed her nose.

"Xiuying and Xiaofan are also arriving today. I haven't told anyone yet because I want us to meet them first." Jinhai smiled.

"What a pity! This should be the happiest day of our lives, but instead, we're worried about Jiayi's life," Xiaosheng huffed. "Those two morons sitting on their thrones have ruined our lives since day one. When's the execution supposed to happen?"

"Today. At sunset." *Might as well let it all out.*

"And... and when are Xiuying and Xiaofan supposed to arrive?" Xiaosheng probed.

"Probably in the next three to four hours, but I can't say for sure. You know how tough voyages are."

"I really hope they make it. It just feels like the Universe is against us right now."

"Don't say that, Sister. It will only get better from here." Jinhai tried to comfort her.

"How can you be so calm during a time like this?!" Xiaosheng shouted.

"As you grow older, you come to realize that even when all the odds are against you, they cannot defeat you unless you allow them to. I learned that from Fia," her brother whispered. "Speaking of Fia, would you like to go visit her? I need to head over to Lixin's." Xiaosheng nodded and extended her hand out for him to take. "Come on. I think we *both* need a good distraction."

CHAPTER
TEN

MEANWHILE, THE OTHER SIDE OF THE CASTLE WAS DRAPED IN darkness. After years of separation, Qianfan and Daiyu were finally back together again. With time, their hearts had turned cold, and they had found solace in torturing others.

"You know what we should do?" Daiyu whistled as she raised her glass of red wine up to her lips. "We should make an example out of this."

"How so?" Qianfan asked, intrigued.

"We should execute the bitch in front of the entire kingdom so that nobody ever tries to conspire against us ever again!" Daiyu cackled. "This will make all the peasants fear us even more."

"I love it! Punish anyone who even dares to utter a word of disrespect to us, slaughter those who dare to stand in our way." Qianfan laughed as he walked back and forth with his fingers wrapped behind his back. Then he whispered to himself, "Fear is the only thing that'll help me keep this crown." He turned to face the door and shouted, "Guard!" One of his loyal guards came rushing in within a second of his bellow, carrying a scroll and quill in his hands. "Start writing," Qianfan ordered him.

"Make it good, my husband. I need everyone to know who's in charge here," Daiyu called out.

The king cleared his throat and began speaking, "Peasants of the Jinu Kingdom, I hereby invite you all to witness our first-ever execution, and I expect you all to be there with bells on. Witness what happens to those to dare defy me, for if you do, it shall forever deter you from going against my orders. Come to the castle at sunset to see justice served! Yours truly, the King of Jinu." The king then waved the guard away. "Oh, wait, one more thing. Those who do not show up will all witness their own executions." He then waved off the guard once more. "Now go! Take the scroll to the harbor and make the official announcement!"

The guard hesitated, but before Qianfan could wave a second time—the fatal wave—he quickly bolted out of the room and ran as fast as he could down the hall and out of the building.

Oblivious to the king's demand, Jinhai and Xiaosheng arrived at Lixin's on the other side of town. Fia was already there, helping Haitao plant new flowers to celebrate the new upcoming year.

"Jinhai! Xiaosheng! What a pleasant surprise! What brings you two here?" Lixin asked with delight.

"Our lives," Xiaosheng murmured with a stale face.

"What happened?"

Haitao and Fia also stopped what they were doing and looked up.

"My father has gone too far. He has imprisoned Jiayi," Jinhai revealed and politely asked everyone to head back inside.

They all settled in the living room with the window open, highlighting a beautiful blue sky and the vast ocean. It was a busy day at the harbor, and they could see local ships departing on their voyages.

"How exactly are you going to confront the king? You can't just walk in and seize the throne. He'll kill you!" Haitao asked after Jinhai finished explaining everything that had been going on.

"Only time can guide us now. But first, I need to focus on meeting my sisters and saving Jiayi," Jinhai firmly stated.

"Your powers can help with saving Jiayi, right?" Fia chimed in and asked.

"Yes, most definitely. Xiaosheng and Jinhai can

both use their powers to help Jiayi escape. Xiuying and Xiaofan can also help them out. Together, they are bound to be invincible," Lixin replied.

"Only if they get here in time," Xiaosheng mumbled, deflated.

"There they are! Look!" Fia jumped up excitedly while pointing toward the tiny ant-sized boats arriving at the harbor. "I recognize the flag of the Baoshu Kingdom!"

"Really? No way!" Xiaosheng stood up and ran toward the window. "They're really here!"

"They are going to arrive any minute now, Jinhai," Haitao said.

"Yes, you both should go meet them. We will wait for you here." Lixin lightly touched Jinhai's shoulder and nodded.

This was really happening! Jinhai's heart was pounding in his chest, and he was feeling so many different emotions all at once. He didn't know what he was going to say to them, how he was going to react to seeing them for the first time, but he left for the harbor with Xiaosheng anyway.

The closer their carriage got to the harbor, the clearer he could see the ships and the flag of Baoshu, and it was a beautiful sight to see. The harbor was crowded with people by the time they arrived, merchants going to and from the island on the one day where the flowers seemed to magically bloom. Luckily, there were so many other ships at the dock that no one seemed to really notice the royal ships arriving, just like Jinhai had wanted.

He stood there with Xiaosheng, heart racing and squeezing her hand, when suddenly, someone around his age came running out and straight toward Xiaosheng.

"Xiaosheng! I can't believe it's you!" the woman cried. "I'm Xiaofan, your sister!"

Xiaosheng started to tear up while tightly hugging her back. Jinhai stood next to them with tears in his eyes as Xiaofan soon let go and hugged him next. "Oh, look at you! You have gotten so big. The last time I saw you, you were just a baby."

Jinhai hugged her back, too choked up to find the right words to say, when he soon saw someone who resembled Xiaofan coming up behind them.

"You must be Xiuying, the eldest," Jinhai said and bowed.

"Oh, no need for formalities, Little Brother. We're all family, and I'm so happy that we are finally all here together." Xiuying beamed and wrapped her arms around Jinhai and Xiaosheng.

"Are we even welcomed here?" Zhang teased as he stepped off the ship.

"Don't think so." Han laughed as they walked toward the four siblings.

"Always have to be the center of attention, don't you?" Xiuying teased back and pulled Zhang to her side. "Jinhai, Xiaosheng, meet Zhang, my husband and the King of Baoshu."

"And this," Xiaofan pulled Han over next to her, "is Han, my fiancé."

"So, lead us to Father." Xiuying clapped her hands together. "It's been so long since I've last seen the man who changed my life forever."

"Not just yet," Jinhai said. "We're going to Lixin's first so we can finalize out plan. Plus, I'd like you all to meet the man who practically raised me."

"Lead the way." Zhang gestured.

As they headed toward the carriages, Jinhai noticed the king's own carriages arriving at the harbor and guards beginning to round up the crowd.

"What's this?" Xiaofan asked.

"I have no idea." Jinhai glanced around, frightened for what was about to happen.

One of the guards started to read from a scroll, and every word made Jinhai's heart stop. Even the guard himself was trembling with the words that he was forced to say, but he had to keep going for the sake of his life. The faces of the crowd turned pale, and not even a whisper graced the air—only shivers of fear and silence.

He was announcing the public execution of Jiayi, not only as a punishment for her, but as a threat of death for all those who failed to obey every order from the king. This was an order to incite fear in the hearts of the people.

"What's happening, Jinhai?" Xiuying asked with trepidation in her voice.

"Jiayi? Isn't that the woman who looked after you and Xiaosheng?" Xiaofan added.

"We need to go. Now! We're running out of time! I need to do everything I can to *not* let this happen." Jinhai nodded.

They all quietly scampered toward the carriages without creating any attention from the crowd. The girls all sat in one carriage while the boys took the other. None of them had a clue as to what was going on, but Zhang was certain of one thing—Jinhai had potential in him, and he was confident that the prince knew what he was doing. To Zhang, Jinhai was born to be a king.

When they arrived, Fia was over the moon to reconnect with Xiaofan and Xiuying, and Lixin greeted them with open arms. Haitao's jaw practically dropped when he saw Xiaofan, and Jinhai knew he had a little crush on her, but he kept his distance. Besides, Han looked strong enough to beat the both of them up.

"Jiayi took care of Xiaosheng when our mother abandoned her at birth, and she also took me under her wing when Father grew ashamed of me and tried to hide me from the rest of the castle. But even still, Daiyu blamed Jiayi for her children hating her, never herself, just like she'd blamed Mei for Xiuying turning against her. So, to make herself feel better, she threw Jiayi in prison, just like she'd done to Mei and Huiqing. Just like Father had killed his own mother for questioning his sickening ways," Jinhai explained.

"I'm not even surprised. Truly, nothing has changed," Xiuying whispered.

"I don't think they'll ever be capable of change," Xiaofan added.

"This is why we need to bring change to this kingdom as soon as possible. Otherwise, more and more people will keep dying." Lixin sighed.

"Good thing Jinhai here is the right man for that!" Haitao exclaimed and threw a wink over at Xiaofan.

"But... but how exactly are we going to save Jiayi?" Xiaosheng stuttered. "I don't want to lose her!"

"We won't let anything happen to her. I will do everything in my power to make sure of it," Zhang assured her.

"You need to get the people on your side, Jinhai," Han told him. "Qianfan is going to fall into his own trap. I doubt any of the townspeople are going to support the execution, and if you can gather the crowd on your side, you might have a chance of stopping him at sunset."

Jinhai was intrigued. "I need to tell them all the truth. If they know just how evil their king is, they will join forces with me. My father isn't unstoppable."

"He's going to think that the public is there to witness the execution, and we will all take him down with the element of surprise." Zhang smirked.

"Zhang, maybe you can accompany Jinhai. For protection," Xiuying suggested.

"Might be better if Han goes. I'm pretty sure your

father still remembers me from the last time I mouthed off to him."

"Agree, and we should leave now before it's too late," Han said.

Xiuying, Zhang, and Fia stayed behind at the house while everyone else headed back toward the harbor to gather the people.

"Jinhai, wait!" Fia called out after him, running up to him and wrapping her arms around him. "Promise me you'll stay safe."

"I'll do everything in my power if it means coming home to see you again." Jinhai pressed his forehead against hers and leaned down to give her a passionate kiss. He wrapped his arms around her waist and pulled her in tightly before letting go again. "The Universe is on my side." He gave her another quick kiss and rushed toward the carriages.

When they reached the harbor, some of the merchants and townspeople were still frightened by the news, whispering sounds of nervousness to everyone who passed them. On the right side of the harbor was a large and menacing bell, a bell that was only rung when tragedy struck the kingdom and the people needed to prepare for war. The group of five walked toward it and stood temere for a second as Jinhai took a deep breath.

"Are you ready?" Han asked.

"Yes," Jinhai whispered as Xiaosheng held onto his hand. "I can do this."

Jinhai then stepped onto the stone pavement and pulled the rope, sounding the bell exactly three times.

Hearing the sound of a bell that was usually never rung, the people at the harbor all stopped and looked over to see the prince. Even those from afar left their homes and ran over to see what the commotion was all about. Within a matter of minutes, the space before them was filled with the people of Jinu.

Jinhai didn't even need to look first before speaking. He knew his father wouldn't leave his precious throne even if the entire kingdom was burning down. Besides, he'd probably just assume that a guard had rung it for the execution.

He stepped forward toward the people and started to speak.

"Beloved people of Jinu, I stand here today with a heavy heart and a confession, a truth that you all deserve to know. The king, my father, has been hiding secrets, and it's about time they come out. As many of you may not even know, I am not the eldest child. I have two older sisters, the princesses of Jinu, both of whom my father sent away to die. And those who helped them? Well, let's just say things didn't turn out very well for them. And then there's me and my younger sister, Xiaosheng. We were both treated like royalty, sure, but we were never really wanted either. Qiang, our grandmother, and Jiayi, the woman about to be executed raised us, and as a result, they are now either dead or destined to die. This just goes to show that anyone who dares to stand in the way of the king and queen will be killed... one way or another, and this needs to stop! I am standing before you today, begging for you to join me in my fight against injustice, begging you to stop allowing my father to treat us like his own personal puppets. He doesn't care about us, any of us, not even his own children. At sunset, right before the execution is set to commence, we will rise and show him who's boss."

CHAPTER
ELEVEN

Jinhai glanced at the crowd, and during those first few minutes of silence, his hope began to shrivel, but then out of the blue, he heard a voice.

"We're with you, Jinhai," one man shouted.

"Time to take down the rotten dictator," another joined in.

And soon, the crowd burst into chants and started cheering for Jinhai. Eventually, everyone else chimed in and started to yell, "Burn, Qianfan, burn!"

Just like Jinhai had wanted.

The sun was almost setting, so Lixin and Haitao

rallied the crowd, and they all began marching toward the castle. There was no panic, no fear, only the determination to save a life.

When they reached the front gate, even the iron bars and army of guards weren't enough to hold them back. The crowd was too big, and people were pushing down everything in their path to get inside. This moment was indeed a revolution, and the enthusiasm of the townspeople was even more impeccable than anyone could've anticipated.

They arrived to the courtyard—where the execution was set to be held—and found Qianfan and Daiyu standing at the center, surrounded by armed guards. Jiayi was down on her knees with her hands tied behind her back and a black silk cloth covering her eyes. The sky had turned a deep orange as the sun slowly faded away, and the gust of wind sent chills down everyone's spines. Evil was certainly in the air.

"What a magnificent turnout!" Qianfan laughed. "It looks like the entire kingdom is here to witness the execution of this filthy animal."

"And look who finally found his place and decided to bring them all here!" Daiyu grinned with pride. "Our bastard of a son!" Then she leaned down. "Oh, Jiayi, how I wish you could see this. Everyone here to watch you die. Guess they really are *my* children after all."

Just as she finished her last word, the crowd started to chant, "Burn, Qianfan, burn! Burn, Daiyu, burn!" The voices grew louder and louder until Jinhai stepped forward to face his parents.

"We know everything. The people here know everything, the abandonment of your daughters and the death of those who once loved you." He raised up his hand and gestured to the crowd. "Do you see all these people around you? They are not here to watch you execute Jiayi; they are here to watch you burn, take you down. And the guards? Ha! You really think they're on your side? They fear you more than they respect you, and once they realize that there's power in numbers, *no one* is going to stop this mob."

Jinhai stared straight into his father's eyes as Qianfan darted his eyes around to the angry hoard that surrounded him. "There's nothing you can do anymore besides walk away... for your own safety. The people no longer fear you," Jinhai finished.

Qianfan felt like a dagger had just been pierced through his heart. Betrayed by his own son. *His own son!* And beside him, Daiyu was trembling for the first time in her life. They both couldn't understand how their plan had failed. It was foolproof! But they remained silent, and their faces pale, they slowly walked back into the castle.

The crowd cheered as Jinhai untied Jiayi from her restraints, and Xiaosheng rushed over to embrace her. She removed the cloth from her eyes and cried into her shoulders.

"I thought I'd never see you again," Jiayi cried.

"I would *never* let anything happen to you!" Xiaosheng exclaimed.

"It's time for us to go," Jinhai whispered and lightly touched Jiayi's shoulder.

"Where?" Jiayi asked.

"Home," Xiaosheng replied.

They all walked off the castle grounds, and the crowd dispersed after wishing Jiayi the best for her life ahead. They walked to the harbor and rode the carriages back to Lixin's house. The ride back was peaceful, the sky had turned dark with infinite stars shining bright, and the aroma of blooming flowers wafted through the air. Xiaosheng stayed with Jiayi and held onto her hand.

"Let's just give them a little scare, shall we?" Han suggested when they arrived. "Tell them our plan had failed and see how they react."

"Diabolical. Let's do it!" Jinhai laughed.

Jiayi stayed in the carriage while the rest entered the house. Xiuying and Fia had decorated it with fresh flowers and oil lamps, and delicious moon cakes were served on the table with a small pot of tea.

"There's nothing to celebrate," Han said in an ominous tone.

"Is this some kind of joke?" Jinhai added.

Fia was the first to stop. "Wait... what? Tell me it's not true."

"How could you let this happen?" Xiuying nearly shouted.

But Zhang remained silent. He could see the faint

smirk on Han's face and knew he was clearly up to something... he just didn't know what.

Jinhai then looked over at Han, and they both started to laugh.

"That's not funny!" Xiuying yelled and gave Han a playful push.

"Really, Jinhai?" Fia darted her eyes over at Jinhai.

"Hey, don't blame me! It was Han's idea." Jinhai raised his hands in the air.

"Me? Everyone knows that I'm not one to play such childish games," Han teased and chuckled as Jiayi was welcomed inside with hugs and kisses.

That night, it truly felt like the entire family was back together again. Haitao and Han did their best to lighten the dark mood with all the jokes they had in their pockets. Xiaofan and Fia caught up with each other after years and years of being apart. And Xiuying went inside the kitchen to brew some more tea, accompanied by her little brother.

"Never in my life did I ever think this day would come," Xiuying pondered. "Look around; this feels like *home.*"

"Home is where your heart is, right?" Jinhai mumbled.

"Right, but in your case, your heart is somewhere else. Inside a very special person, I might say."

"It's not like that." Jinhai blushed.

"She's different. Resilient. Strong. And you love her. I see it all over your face. Why not ask for her hand in marriage?" Xiuying asked.

"Just waiting for the right time, I guess."

"You will always continue waiting if you keep waiting for the right time. The right time is never going to come. You need to make it the right time. And besides, with how things are going in this kingdom, the right time is running out." She turned to face her brother. "If you feel like you are ready, just go for it."

"You're right. I *am* ready." Jinhai nodded and started to tear up.

"What happened?" Xiuying asked.

"It's just that... I've never had an older sibling to help me through life. My entire life, I've felt like I've had to be strong and stay brave for the sake of Xiaosheng. It just feels like such a relief to know that all the burden isn't just on my shoulders, and that I have someone to turn to in times of need. It's something I've been missing my whole life."

"My only wish is that I could've been here sooner. So much has been taken away from us," Xiuying mused.

"We just have to make up for lost times." Jinhai grinned, and they both walked back out with two fresh pots of tea.

Jinhai felt a comforting warmth inside his heart. He felt protected, supported, but at the same time, he knew his father wouldn't just give up. He was planning something; he could feel it. Tomorrow, they would all go visit Qianfan. After the humiliation that he'd put his father through today, he was terrified of what would come next.

"I bet everyone in town is celebrating the major win from today. We should go join them!" Xiaofan said after taking her first hot sip.

"Totally! We should all be there, especially Jiayi," Xiaosheng added.

"Let's go! I can't wait to stuff my face with everyone's delicious baked goods." Haitao jumped up.

"You all can go ahead. I'm feeling a bit tired. I might just turn in early," Fia said as she yawned.

"I'll stay with you, keep you company," Jinhai said to Fia.

"Perfect! We shall leave you two alone," Xiuying said and gave Jinhai a quick wink.

"We also need to stop by the ship. All our belongings are still in there," Xiaofan reminded everyone.

"Your wish is my command," Han replied as they all marched out of the house and boarded the carriages.

The house became silent after they left, leaving Fia and Jinhai alone. Fia stood up and began cleaning up the porcelain dishes and cups.

"Are you still upset from what happened earlier?" Jinhai asked.

"Maybe," Fia whispered.

"It wasn't my idea," Jinhai insisted.

"Maybe."

"Do you need any help with that?" Jinhai asked as Fia started to wash the dishes inside the kitchen.

"Maybe."

He walked up to the sink and stood beside her. "I'm sorry."

"Maybe." Fia giggled.

"What does that even mean?" Jinhai asked with a chuckle.

"It just means maybe, a possibility," Fia replied.

"So... will you marry me then?" Jinhai asked, shyly looking away. "Maybe?"

"Yes," she said, her eyes locked on the floor.

"Is that for the maybe or for the question?"

"For the question!" Fia laughed, and Jinhai pulled her in for a long hug.

THE MOMENT QIANFAN ENTERED BACK INTO THE CASTLE, THE only thing he could feel was humiliation. Embarrassment!

"The audacity of that stupid child!" he yelled and hurled his sword toward the mirror, shattering both the glass and his reflection.

Daiyu, on the other hand, was finding herself back in a similar situation, caught between her children and husband, but this time, she had already picked a side, and there was no turning back.

"He is going to regret *ever* crossing me!" the king shouted.

"Qianfan, you need to calm down," Daiyu whispered in a soft voice.

"No! How can you even *think* about calming down

during a time like this? This is *war*, and our foolish son has declared it. Does he really think rallying a bunch of peasants can help him seize the throne? No! I have everything. I have the magic stone, a power that nobody else has! He is a fool to have crossed me. If it means bloodshed to keep the throne, then let it be. He has no idea what he has gotten himself into!" Qianfan bellowed and stormed down the hallway, smashing anything and everything that stood in his way.

To Daiyu, the situation was out of control. It was one thing when the chaos remained within the walls of the castle, but having the public turn against them was unacceptable. It was something that their ancestors had never faced, and to make it worse, it was provoked by their own children. Such shame!

Qianfan's heart had turned stone cold over the years, and the only emotions he felt were ones that drained his ability to channel his power. The negativity inside of him took away his greatness. Even the love that he used to have for his wife had now dissipated, the one emotion that made him who he was in the first place.

The only power he had now was the magic stone. The magic stone was the main source of energy for all the elements in the Universe, even the ones unknown to humankind. The one who held the stone was the most powerful because the powers could be unleashed with just the mind, regardless of emotions. For that very reason, the stone was kept inside the royal chamber, locked away from everyone who walked within the castle walls, and the only person who could ever access it was the king himself.

THE NEXT MORNING, JINHAI WOKE UP TO THE SCENIC VIEW OF the ocean, colorful flowers in bloom, and best of all, all the people he loved. But as much as he wanted to remain in bed and bask in the moment, he suddenly remembered what day it was—the day that the king would reunite with the daughters he'd abandoned and face the wrath of the son he'd so desperately wanted then also kicked aside. Sure, he felt guilty turning against his father. As a child, all he'd ever wanted was for his father to love him, accept him. But what other choice did he have? Let Qianfan destroy the kingdom and kill the people of Jinu? He couldn't let that happen!

"You missed the fun party last night, Jinhai. The townspeople are such wonderful people! We danced, we sang, and we ate some of the best food I've ever had in my life. It was such a delight!" Zhang exclaimed.

"We missed you," Xiuying said with a smile on her face. "It would've been fun to have our little brother out with us."

"And we also visited the main market. What a place! Things have definitely changed around here over the years," Xiaofan chimed in.

"With time, things change. It happens," Han replied, holding onto Xiaofan's hand.

"I need to tell you all something very important," Jinhai announced, changing the topic. He then gestured his hand toward Fia. "Can I have you by my side?" Fia gladly took his proffered hand and stood beside him. "Last night, I proposed to Fia."

"And?" Xiaosheng asked sarcastically, already knowing the answer given the massive smile on Fia's face.

"We're getting married!" Jinhai cheered excitedly and swung Fia's hand into the air.

"I knew it!" Xiaofan screamed and ran up to hug her little brother.

"Congratulations!" Xiuying sang and joined into the hug.

"Leave some space for me!" Xiaosheng whined as she squeezed her way in.

"We are *definitely* going to have the wedding before we leave," Xiaofan said. "If that's okay with you two."

"Of course!" Fia agreed. "I wouldn't have it any other way."

Jiayi then remembered a vital piece of information that Huiqing had revealed to her in prison. He used to be Qianfan's closest confidant and knew about the magic stone. "Jinhai, there is something you should know. The magic stone. It's locked inside the royal chamber, the same stone that was used to mark you and your sisters, and the very stone that gave you all your powers. However, the stone is more powerful than all of you combined, and it contains every single one of your powers plus much, much more." Then she swallowed hard. "And Qianfan has it."

Jinhai gulped, and he felt his confidence begin to dwindle. He was so sure that with the help of his sisters, he could take down the king. But after knowing this, after knowing that Qianfan was still more powerful than all of them combined, made him start to doubt whether his plan could actually be successful. He was afraid, but he knew they had all come too far to back down.

"It's okay, Jiayi," he assured her. "There is nothing to worry about. I can handle this."

Jiayi smiled as she touched Jinhai's face with motherly affection. "I hope so."

"But just to be on the safe side, maybe you should touch some wood," Haitao said.

"I don't think that's how it works—" Jinhai began.

"Just touch it!" Xiaosheng exclaimed.

Shrugging his shoulders, Jinhai bent down and touched the wooden floor. "Whatever you say."

"You could have touched the door," Xiaofan said.

"That's for the weak," Xiaosheng mumbled with a snort.

"Alright!" Jinhai clapped his hands together. "The wood has been touched. Now we head to the castle."

TWELVE

THE GATES OF THE CASTLE OPENED WIDE, AND ALL THE horrific memories of her childhood came rushing back into Xiuying's mind. She remembered the carriage ride that sent her away for good, the carriage ride that was meant to kill her. To this day, nightmares continued to haunt her, and even though she'd sworn that she would never return to the place that ruined her life, she continued to find herself back here over and over for the sake of her siblings.

"You are not weak. Remember what you came here

for," Zhang comforted her when he noticed his wife's eyes tearing up.

By the time their carriages arrived at the main entrance, the guards had already informed the king and queen of the unexpected visit. Qianfan had taken the stone out of the chamber and placed it at the center of his crown.

"It doesn't even smell the same anymore, but it still reminds me of my awful childhood," Xiaofan said as they entered and looked around, taking it all in. It's all a reality now. The place that was meant to be their home now felt so foreign and unwanted.

Suddenly, they heard footsteps storming toward the entrance and saw Qianfan approaching them, with Daiyu draped around his right arm.

"Here we go," Han joked in a low voice.

"Not now, Han," Xiaofan whistled.

Jinhai noticed the magic stone sitting on the king's crown, and he knew his father had a plan—or a trick—up his sleeve. He was going to fight them, fire with fire, or he'd die trying.

"The stone. It's in his crown. We need to get it away from him; otherwise, we don't stand a chance," Jinhai whispered.

"How many times will it take to get rid of you all for good?" Qianfan yelled when he saw the faces of his children.

"What is this? Sabotage?" Daiyu asked.

"There is no need to be upset or draw weapons. We can discuss this like adults," Xiuying politely said.

"We are here to give our family a chance, but only if Father steps down from the throne and hands the crown over to Jinhai. The time has come, Father. You are getting old, and the kingdom needs a new king," Xiaofan added.

"Are you serious?" Daiyu laughed. "Do you really think Qianfan is just going to hand over everything he'd worked so hard for? Everything that he deserves? You were right, my husband. Such foolish souls. I pity them." Then she spat on the ground.

"And you? You little brat!" Qianfan hissed, pointing at Xiaofan. "You think I can't handle the responsibilities of being King? And who can? Your overly emotional brother who acts more like a princess than a prince?"

"You will only ever get the crown in your dreams," Daiyu taunted.

"Now leave!" Qianfan ordered.

"We are not leaving without the crown. The throne is Jinhai's, and the people of this kingdom do not want you as their king," Xiuying said sternly and stood her ground.

"Yet Jinhai is letting all the women advocate for him. Only a *weak* man uses women as a shield. He wasn't powerful enough to take the throne himself, so he had to call on his sisters. What a joke!" Qianfan blurted with a loud laugh.

"I'd much rather have someone who relies on his family to be the king than someone who abandons them. You're no leader, Father. You are a dictator. A *monster*," Xiaofan declared.

"Monster? A monster? How dare you speak to your father—your king—in such disrespectful manner?!" Fury filled Qianfan's eyes, and within seconds, his hands turned into fire, and he threw a fireball straight at Xiaofan.

However, before it could hit her, Han pushed her out of the way, injuring himself instead.

"Han!" Xiaofan shouted, running over to treat the minor wound.

"Are you out of your mind?" Xiuying screamed at Qianfan.

"Qianfan, let me make this very clear to you. We both know that my army is much larger than yours, and as we speak, I have three ships docked at your harbor filled with armed guards and the most powerful weapons that this world has ever seen. Attack one of my own again, and I can have them all here with the snap of a finger," Zhang stated and slowly walked toward Qianfan with his sword.

"Nobody threatens me in my own kingdom!" Qianfan bellowed, ready to shower Zhang with enough fireballs to kill him. But nothing came out... nor did his hands light up. "What?" He reached his hands up to feel around his head but also came up empty. It was no longer there!

Then he saw it. From the corner of his left eye, he saw his precious crown floating in the air, finding its way on top of Jinhai's head with the help of Xiaosheng and her newfound power.

"Whoever possesses this crown is King, to me and to everyone else," Xiaosheng declared with a smirk on her face.

"You little prick! I knew there was a reason I've always hated you!" Daiyu screamed and turned to her husband. "Do something, Qianfan! Use your power. Kill them! We need to kill them all!"

But despite his wife's cries, his dear wife whom he used to do anything for, Qianfan could not hear a thing. His mind and body had both grown numb, and for the first time in decades, he felt like he was losing control. He knew he'd been defeated, that his last hope for victory was now sitting on the head of his one and only son. His vision grew blurry, his arms grew weak, and all of a sudden, he vanished into thin air, as if someone had snatched him away.

For a minute or two, no one understood what had happened, but the longer they waited, the more evident it became that he was not coming back. Their nightmare was finally over.

As for Daiyu, she no longer had the king to hide behind, and she soon faced her own nightmare of being completely alone and surrounded by all the children whom she'd tossed aside.

"Please, forgive me," Daiyu pleaded. "Have mercy, for I *am* your mother, after all."

"You were *never* our mother. You've never stood up

for any of us against that evil husband of yours," Xiaofan hissed.

"You showed no mercy to Mei, so why should we show mercy to you?" Xiuying jeered.

"And don't forget about what you didn't show to Jiayi," Xiaosheng added resentfully.

"Guards, please take Daiyu to the prison, and lock her in the same room that Mei and Jiayi were kept, so that she will forever remember what she had done. And I want all the other prisoners set free, especially Huiqing. They do not deserve to be in there a second longer," Jinhai ordered.

Xiaosheng came running toward her brother once he finished his order. "We are finally free! No longer will we have to live in fear."

"Thanks to you!" Xiaofan hugged Xiaosheng.

"You saved the day, Little Sister," Xiuying agreed.

"Little one's a champ," Han said appreciatively.

"She sure is." Zhang smiled.

"You know what we need? A proper ceremony! To inaugurate Jinhai as the new King of Jinu!" Xiaofan suggested.

"Yes!" Xiaosheng shouted excitedly.

"Is that really necessary?" Jinhai asked humbly.

"We wouldn't have it any other way," Xiuying whispered beside him. "And as the eldest, it would be my honor to crown you."

A few minutes later, the guards brought Huiqing into the room. He was old, weak, and had trouble walking on his own, but when he saw Xiuying, he couldn't contain his feelings.

"My child, you are here!" he exclaimed when he saw her. "I never thought I would ever see you again." He placed his hand on Xiuying's head. She struggled to find words through all the happiness that she was feeling... so she didn't.

"Thank you for all that you have done, Huiqing," Zhang said while shaking his hand. "If it weren't for you, Xiuying would not be alive today."

"I am so sorry that you had to spend your life in prison because of me. If I had known about this, I would've done my best to free you," Xiuying finally said, gasping for air.

"No, my child. This was all in the Universe's plan. It was all to bring you and your sister back to Jinu and save the kingdom." Huiqing smiled. "Everything worked out like it was supposed to."

"Huiqing, I want you to know that I have cleared your name to the public. That you were mistreated and wronged. And," Jinhai cleared his throat, "I would like to reinstate your position as Chief of the Military. It would be an honor to have someone like you protecting this kingdom."

"Thank you, my child." Huiqing bowed. "I knew I've always liked you."

"What happened?" Jiayi rushed in, interrupting the conversation.

"Where are your parents?" Fia asked.

"Is everything okay?" Haitao added.

"Once voice at a time, please!" Han laughed.

Xiaosheng sat them all down and started to explain everything that had happened. Once she finished, Jiayi said, "I still don't understand Qianfan's disappearance."

"Urban legend has it," Lixin started with a deep voice, "that when evil spirits realize their wrongdoings, their souls are taken by the dark shadows of Hell, trapped and tortured for eternity. For centuries, criminals and dictators have disappeared without a trace. The same thing must've happened to Qianfan."

"Wow...," Xiaofan said. "And I've always thought those legends were all just stories. Nothing more."

"Oh, whatever! We have more important things to focus on today," Xiaosheng exclaimed. "We need to prepare for the crowning ceremony!"

Xiaofan chuckled. "You're right. I'll get all the castle maids to start preparing."

As Jinhai watched his loved ones around him, he finally felt like he was home. Despite everything that had happened in this castle and all the trauma he'd dealt with as a child, things were finally looking up, and he no longer feared living inside these very walls.

EPILOGUE

Jɪɴʜᴀɪ's ɪɴᴀᴜɢᴜʀᴀᴛɪᴏɴ ᴡᴀs ᴄᴇʟᴇʙʀᴀᴛᴇᴅ ʟɪᴋᴇ ᴀɴʏ ᴏᴛʜᴇʀ traditional holiday. He wanted it to remain small and close-knit, only inviting those within the walls of the kingdom. Qianfan was always focused on trying to impress the other kings, but Jinhai cared more about impressing his own people. In Jinhai's kingdom, nobody slept under an open sky or with an empty stomach, and he completely abolished the one-child rule in Jinu so that little girls born no longer had to be killed or sent away in hopes of having a boy.

A week after the ceremony, Jinhai and Fia got

married, and the kingdom now had a wise and empathetic queen. Jiayi and Xiaosheng lived with them in the royal chamber, and they continued eating their meals together, just like old times. Jinhai offered Haitao and Lixin their own place at the castle, but they refused and insisted on staying inside their own house. Huiqing was given a piece of land and sacks of gold coins to start his new life, and he eventually reunited with his family once Jinhai cleared his name.

Xiuying and Zhang left after the wedding to head back to Baoshu, and a week later, Jinhai received a scroll that Xiuying was expecting her first child, a little girl. Han took Xiaofan back to Shénhuà, but only after he vowed to Jinhai that Shénhuà would become Jinu's trusted ally during times of conflict and war.

As for Daiyu, she stayed within the confined walls of prison, accompanied by silence and loneliness. She had everything that she needed physically—food, water, and warm blankets—but her mind continued eating at her with each passing day with one unanswered question.

Was it the legend that made Qianfan disappear? Or did he finally manage to generate his own black magic spell that he used on himself?

That's a question that no one would ever be able to answer, and Qianfan was a man whom everyone hoped would never return.

The End

About the Author

Viola Tempest is a dystopian fantasy and paranormal romance author who yearns to expose the truth of those in the modern world: the good, the bad, and the ugly. Her inspiration primarily stems from life experiences, those who annoy her, ex-boyfriends, and the crazy dreams that pop into her head every once in a while.

The Righteous Son

THE LOST DAUGHTERS TRILOGY BOOK THREE

VIOLA TEMPEST

www.ingramcontent.com/pod-product-compliance
Lightning Source LLC
Chambersburg PA
CBHW030146010826
48973CB00002B/748